COMANCHE MOON

The Reverend Jonas Faulkner, pastor of the First Claremont Presbyterian Church in Texas, is a man with a secret: in his younger days he was a notorious gunman, involved in a crime which resulted in the deaths of several children. So when six young girls, travelling to an orphanage in Claremont, are seized by a Kiowa raiding party, Pastor Faulkner knows he must act in atonement for his past sins. For the elderly clergyman is still a force to be reckoned with . . .

SIMON WEBB

COMANCHE MOON

Complete and Unabridged

LINFORD
Leicester

First published in Great Britain in 2013 by
Robert Hale Limited
London

First Linford Edition
published 2015
by arrangement with
Robert Hale Limited
London

A catalogue record for this book is available
from the British Library.

ISBN 978–1–4448–2539–8

Published by
F. A. Thorpe (Publishing)
Anstey, Leicestershire

Set by Words & Graphics Ltd.
Anstey, Leicestershire
Printed and bound in Great Britain by
T. J. International Ltd., Padstow, Cornwall

This book is printed on acid-free paper

1

On a warm day in the summer of 1868, the Reverend Jonas Faulkner was kneeling in the chapel of the Claremont Orphans' Asylum. The words he was saying over and over again were nothing remarkable for a man of his profession in such a place: 'Lord, have mercy upon me, a sinner.' He repeated the prayer one final time and then stood up, gave a last look around the place to make sure it was all in order and walked out; a tall, spare man in his mid-fifties, who looked as though he had a good deal on his mind.

Now the truth is, most ministers proclaim such words as this from time to time. Why, they're straight out of the Good Book; Luke 18:13. Only thing is, the majority of preachers don't sound as though they mean them. Sure, they talk about what big sinners they are, but they say it in such a holy and self-satisfied way that you know they really think of themselves as pretty fine fellows. Reverend Faulkner, though, when he talked of being a sinner, you had the uneasy feeling that he meant it and that his sins might amount to more than the occasional covetous glance at some pretty widow. He sounded like the genuine article: a man who knows about sin.

A few words might not come amiss at this point about Jonas Faulkner. Some ministers, they are obsessed with denouncing loose women, whoring, gambling, strong drink and suchlike. Reverend Faulkner, he never concerned himself overmuch about such matters. His main aim in life was to impress upon the congregation of the First Presbyterian Church of Claremont that it was their God-given duty to care for the helpless and unprotected, especially widows and children. Children in Claremont would come up to him in the street to talk of their troubles and

Reverend Faulkner, he just squatted down as though he were a child himself, listening to them gravely like they were his only business, which in a sense, they were. Faulkner was also a trustee of the local orphans' asylum, which is how our story begins. Because he was praying earnestly to the Lord, on that particular afternoon, being anxious about a group of children who should already have arrived in town and for whom he was making provision in the orphanage.

There is one more thing that we should note about this preacher before we continue, and that is this. Until he was nigh-on forty years of age, Jonas Faulkner had been a notorious hard drinker and famous gunman. He was once renowned across three states for his drinking, cursing and profanity, as well as for an alarming propensity to shoot out of hand any man foolish enough to get crosswise to him.

It is nothing to the purpose of our tale to relate the details of what chanced in Faulkner's life to transform a heavy-drinking, blasphemous and murderous ruffian into the pious and devout man we saw kneeling in that chapel. It is enough to know that he had been the pastor of the Presbyterian Church for better than ten years and was known as the most upright, trustworthy and God-fearing man in the town. Not one person in Claremont knew anything of Pastor Faulkner's early life. Not that he had lied about it or made any attempt at concealment; he just did not encourage questions about his past and clammed up altogether when the subject of his years before becoming a minister happened to come up in the course of conversation.

Jonas Faulkner looked up and down the street as he walked out of the orphanage, before glancing up at the windows opposite. He did this from long habit and not because he really expected anybody to take a shot at him from some concealed position. He was

4

starting to be seriously concerned about the six young girls who were travelling to Claremont from the town of Oneida, about ninety miles south of Claremont. The orphanage there was closing down and the children were being dispersed elsewhere. Two girls of thirteen, three of twelve and an 11-year-old were supposed to have arrived three days ago and Faulkner was thinking that something must have gone wrong. The telegraph did not run between those two small towns at that time, Texas being a bit backwards in that respect compared to some parts of the country to the east and north. The fact that there was practically a war being waged in the north of the state didn't exactly help with communications, either.

He reached Main Street and a boy raced up to him, saying breathlessly, 'Pastor, there's two men to see you. They're waiting at your house. Your housekeeper sent me to find you.'

Faulkner laid his hand gently on

10-year-old Billy's head and smiled at him. 'I declare, Billy Wilson, you do get taller every time I set eyes on you. Thank you for the message and I shall make sure to look out for you in church on Sunday.'

The boy scuffed his foot in the dust, plainly embarrassed. 'My step-pa doesn't like me spending time in church. He wants me to work on Sundays.'

'I shall speak to him,' said Reverend Faulkner quietly. 'I shall set him straight on the road and he will then allow you to come to Sunday School again.'

The boy smiled. 'Are you sure, Reverend?'

'I am sure,' said Faulkner, with complete confidence. 'I shall reason with him.'

Few things irked Jonas Faulkner more than folk working children too hard or not tending properly to their needs. He made a mental note to call on the boy's stepfather and set him on the right path.

The Reverend Faulkner's housekeeper had made the two visitors comfortable in the front parlour, although not without some misgivings. She was not sure that a soldier and a dirty-looking half-breed scout really rated such a courtesy. Maybe, she thought, it would have been more fitting to let them wait in the kitchen.

Faulkner greeted the two men, who both stood up as he entered the room, with a terrible foreboding in his heart, a foreboding that became a sharp fear as soon as the blue-coated cavalryman spoke.

'We understand, sir, that you are expecting a party of children to arrive here soon?'

'What has befallen them? Tell me quickly, Captain.'

'The worst possible, Reverend. The wagons carrying them were ambushed by a band of Kiowa some fifty miles south from here. One of the scouts was killed, as were the men accompanying the children. The two women were, as I

7

understand it, spared. They and the children were taken prisoner. The other scout escaped with his life. This is him.' The captain indicated the raggedy figure standing nearby.

Jonas Faulkner strode up to the scout angrily. He looked so fierce that the mean-looking man flinched and stepped back, as though he feared a blow. 'You cur,' said Faulkner. 'You let a party of helpless children fall into the hands of those bloodthirsty savages? You ran away and left them to their fate? What sort of man are you? Are you not ashamed?'

The man cringed away from the angry minister, responding to the barrage of questions by mumbling something about a man having to look after his own self first. Faulkner turned to the cavalryman. 'What steps will the army take to rescue these children?' he asked.

The soldier seemed uncomfortable to be put on the spot. 'Well, Padre, it's not a simple matter. But I can tell you that we are going to spare no efforts — '

Faulkner cut in. 'Where are these girls now? Are you sure that they are still alive?'

'From all that we can apprehend, they have been traded on by the Indians to a band of Comancheros. These are men who exchange goods with the — '

'I'll warrant I know more about Comancheros than you do yourself, Captain, or are ever likely to. Do you know the location of this group, or what they intend to do with their captives?'

'My guess would be that they will try and ransom them.'

'Ransom! These are penniless orphans. What will happen when they realize that there is no money to be made in that way?'

The captain looked down at the carpet. 'There is a market in girls, particularly young girls, by which I mean virgins. There are brothels in Mexico which are noted for this.'

Jonas Faulkner stared at the captain, putting that uncomfortable individual in mind of some prophet from the Old Testament. 'Will the army act to rescue these children?'

'It would take a troop of regular soldiers and probably a couple of field guns to deal with those Comancheros and their Indian friends where they are currently situated. We think they are now holed up in the Palo Duro Canyon. It is nigh on impossible to mount an assault there without launching a war. One of these days, we might have the men and equipment to achieve this end, but that day is not yet.'

'It is plain to me,' said Reverend Faulkner, 'that there is a deal more cowardice in the world than when I myself was a young man.' The soldier reddened, blushing to his ears like a schoolgirl. Reverend Faulkner ignored this and asked, 'If they were to be ransomed, what would be the value set upon them, do you think?'

The captain considered for a moment. 'Young white girls, such as have not lain before with a man? I would be surprised if they would let them go for less than five hundred dollars apiece, maybe more.'

'Three thousand in total? I doubt that I could raise this sum. We shall see. Where is this nest of Comancheros to be found?' The captain gave a vague location, somewhere in the Palo Duro Canyon, near to a Comanche settlement. Faulkner nodded and then turned on his heel and left the room, without bidding either of the two men goodbye. It was clear that he was deeply distressed at their news, as well as being mightily displeased with them personally. In the hall, as he was picking up his wide-brimmed black hat, he met his housekeeper. 'Have I not always told you, Mrs O'Hara, that if you want a job to be done, you needs must do it yourself? Perhaps you would give those two men a bite to eat? Thank you.' Having said this, he left the house and headed to the home of one of the church elders.

As he walked along the street, the Reverend Faulkner turned the question over in his mind. He concluded, reluctantly, that he would be lucky to raise three hundred dollars, let alone three thousand. Looks to me, he thought to himself, that I shall have to undertake this matter myself, which is not at all a convenient business with so much to do right now. Still and all, there it is.

It must be mentioned here that if any man in town could have extracted three thousand dollars from the citizens of Claremont, the Reverend Faulkner was the man for the job. He was famous among his parishioners for never taking 'No' for an answer where some philanthropic project was involved, such as the orphans' asylum. He had an uncanny knack for divining when anybody had some unexpected sum of money on hand. Let a woman receive an inheritance from some distant relative or a man have a good win at poker and as sure as God made little apples, Reverend Faulkner would be on the doorstep the next day, claiming some of the money for the widow and orphan. He did not mince his words, either, and showed them by many passages in scripture just where their duty lay. He had once laid into one man, a member of his congregation, with the utmost ferocity and given it as his opinion that any person who could win over two hundred and fifty dollars at cards and then not part with a tenth of it towards the upkeep of orphaned children had no business attending church and representing himself as a Christian.

There were respectable folk in that town who tried to pretend they were not at home when Jonas Faulkner was on the prowl for money; sitting quiet in their houses and not answering when he knocked at the door, like people who are avoiding a tradesman to whom they owe money. More than one person had observed that being shaken down by Reverend Faulkner was mighty similar to being held up and robbed by a ruthless and determined bandit.

On this occasion, though, Faulkner knew that he would be unable to raise such a sum of money by his usual means. He walked along, deep in thought, until he came to a smart, prosperous-looking, three-storey house. This was the home of Martin Catchpole, the most important of the church elders. He took the steps at a brisk trot and rapped the knocker vigorously.

Having been ushered into the presence of Catchpole, Reverend Faulkner saw at once that two other elders were present, which made his job a little easier. The three men in the room, who were probably hatching some new business plan relating to building or commerce, were the most influential members of the church. They were also big wheels in Claremont's business community. He greeted them humbly and proceeded to cause utter amazement by saying, 'Gentlemen, I find that I shall be taking a short vacation and I wished to let you know before I left.'

This news was greeted with looks of

astonishment. Jonas Faulkner taking a vacation? As soon expect the moon to go on holiday or the river to take itself off to another state for a fortnight! Faulkner noted their incredulity, saying stiffly, 'I am not in the habit of taking leave of you in this way. I am sorry if it is not quite convenient.'

'Jonas,' said Martin Catchpole, 'you have not taken a break in these ten years or more. You are surely welcome to do so. Where do you propose to go?'

Faulkner had got out of the practice of deceiving others and felt at a loss. The truth, however, would not answer on this occasion. He racked his brains to think of what he and his fellow roughnecks would have done many years previously if they wanted a break. Inspiration came to him. 'I will go to a nearby town and . . . and sit there relaxing. You know, taking it easy with . . . with a drink in my hand . . . ' he tailed off lamely, as well he might.

Reverend Faulkner's almost fanatical abstinence from intoxicating liquor was legendary in Claremont. There were maiden ladies taking half a glass of wine at Christmas who were confirmed drunkards in comparison with Jonas Faulkner.

The three elders looked at their minister in some alarm. The thought of this sober, hard-working and God-fearing preacher unwinding with a glass of whiskey was so at odds with all they knew of the man that it made them think that perhaps he really was in urgent need of a vacation. Relaxing with a drink in his hand indeed! Whatever had prompted this request, it seemed that a break might be what their pastor needed. Catchpole asked, 'When will you be leaving?'

'In half an hour,' was the surprising answer. There was nothing more to be said and try as they might, the three men could get nothing further from Faulkner, other than that he 'needed to get away for a few days'.

Back at his house, Jonas Faulkner went up into the attic and dragged out an old trunk, which he had not looked at since the day he was appointed minister. He opened the lid, removed some papers and books and then reached out a bundle wrapped in a piece of greasy cloth. He untied it and laid the contents on the floor in front of him. There was a Navy Colt revolver, a flask of powder, wadding, lead balls, a tin of copper percussion caps, a can of oil and a nine-inch-long, razor-sharp Bowie knife in a tooled leather sheath.

Faulkner poured a little of the powder from the flask into the palm of his hand and sniffed it, as though it were snuff. Evidently satisfied, he stripped down the pistol, looking down the barrel and oiling the spindle that the cylinder sat on. He worked the trigger a few times and spun the cylinder to see how easy it was moving. Then he loaded the revolver by charging the chambers with powder and adding fragments of lint and lead balls, after which he fitted percussion caps over each of the six nipples and tested the cylinder to see that it was spinning smoothly. From another part of the attic, he dragged an old saddle roll, containing a blanket. He tucked the loaded pistol into the middle of the saddle roll and carried the rest of the materials into his bedroom and loaded them into a leather bag.

Once in his room, the minister sharpened the Bowie knife on the leather strop that he used for his razor. When he had finished, he tested it on the palm of his hand. It was as sharp as an open razor. He took off his belt and threaded the sheath through it and then fixed it so that it was hanging behind him, concealed by his jacket. He practised reaching back and drawing it out a few times.

Faulkner then went in search of his housekeeper, Mrs O'Hara. He commissioned her to put together some bread, cheese and cold meat for him to take on a short journey. He saw no occasion to tell her further on the matter; he did not wish for the news to spread like wildfire throughout the entire town and all the neighbouring farms. Having made all these preparations, he set off to the livery stable, carrying his saddle roll and two large leather bags containing provisions enough to sustain him for a few days.

Jenny, his piebald mare, was held at livery until he had need of her for visiting around the outlying farms. He saddled her up, told the fellow in charge that he would be gone for up to a week and then, with no more ado, he trotted out of Claremont, heading south in the general direction of Palo Duro.

It felt strange to be on the scout again after all these years. He may well have been about the Lord's work these days, but there was still that old familiar feeling: a gun near at hand and only his own wits to rely upon. He would have to see if fifteen years or so of preaching had done anything to dull those wits and make him apt to fall into unexpected danger.

The first danger that the Reverend Faulkner encountered was not at all in the nature of an unexpected hazard. In those first few years after the end of the war, there were many fiddle-footed young men who took to earning a living as road agents, more commonly known as highwaymen. They preyed on lone and vulnerable travellers, stopping them and stealing their money, horse or anything else worth taking. Sometimes, they would band together to tackle bigger game: stagecoaches or even railroad trains. Most, though, like the young man on foot who jumped out in front of Reverend Faulkner some two hours along the road, went for single persons, almost always those who looked as though they would not be able to put up much of a fight. An elderly man in clerical garb must have seemed an ideal target for this young man.

'Hold fast and get off your horse!' cried the boy, who could not have been more than seventeen or eighteen. He emphasized the words by brandishing a revolver and waving it around wildly.

'Take a care of that pistol now, son,' said the Reverend Faulkner as he dismounted.

'Don't you set mind to nothing 'cept handing over your money.'

Faulkner looked apologetic. 'Well, boy, I am not overloaded with cash.' He reached into the inside pocket of his black, broadcloth coat and then, swivelling round, he kicked sharply upward, knocking the gun from the boy's hand. It had clearly been cocked, because it went off at once, the ball whistling past Jenny's head. Before his foot was back on the ground, Faulkner had reached into his saddle roll and pulled out his own revolver, cocking it with his thumb as he did so.

The would-be road agent stood nursing his hand and staring with a look of comical dismay at the sight of his supposed victim drawing down on him with a pistol. 'Don't shoot, mister, I didn't mean no harm to you.'

21

'You surely have a strange way of showing your good intentions,' said Reverend Faulkner grimly: 'I hope I have not hurt your hand too badly?'

'I think you broke my wrist!'

'I hope not. Show me, here.' Faulkner examined the boy's hand. 'The wrist's just sprained, but I am afraid that I have broken your middle finger there. I am sorry for that, but you are fortunate not to have got worse.'

'I thought you was a preacher, in that black outfit and all.'

'What a mercy you chose me and not some fellow with a bad temper. You will live. I would earnestly entreat you to turn aside from this path, though. I do not think that you are equipped for such a lively line of work. If a man my age can best you, the Lord only knows what will become of you if you come up against some younger and more aggressive person. Give it up, son, while you are still able.'

Having delivered himself of this helpful advice, and still keeping the young man covered with his pistol, the Reverend Faulkner remounted, touched his hat to the boy and rode off.

It was dark when Jonas Faulkner decided to stop for the night. He didn't feel the need for a fire and so just unrolled his blanket and settled down. First, though, he prayed to the Lord, speaking the words out loud, as he found that focused his mind better.

'Dear Lord, you have set me on a strange trail today and one which I could not have foreseen. Still, your ways are not the ways of man and so I should not have been too surprised, I guess.

'I do not know what is to be the end of this enterprise and that is a fact. Seems to me that you would have done better to choose a younger man for the job, although I am not complaining. Perhaps a jaunt of this sort will do me good. I hope, Lord, that you will set a watch upon my housekeeper, who is a faithful servant of yours. I would also like you to soften the heart of Billy Wilson's step-pa and let him see that it is not the thing to keep a child working all day on a Sunday. Oh, and perhaps you might venture to whisper to that young fellow as I encountered earlier and advise him to choose a new career. He is surely too innocent and trusting for to be a road agent. Imagine seeing a man of my age wearing a black coat, and taking it as licence to rob the fellow with impunity. I would not like him to meet a person who is less forgiving than me. I ask these things in your son's name. Amen.'

Following this, Reverend Faulkner snuggled down for the night and slept like a babe until dawn.

2

Before we pick up our story again where we left off, with Pastor Faulkner sleeping rough for the first time in over fifteen years, we need to say a few words about the people called Comancheros, who, as you will recall, now had a hold of the six young girls from the Oneida orphanage. Claremont and Oneida were in northern Texas, not too far from New Mexico. Some years earlier, the Comanches had driven out the Apaches from that region and established themselves, along with the Kiowa, in New Mexico and parts of Texas. Their big stronghold was near a network of canyons known as Palo Duro.

Palo Duro was a regular maze of canyons, gullies, cliffs, caves, ravines and blind ends. It stretched for miles and it was easy enough to get lost once you entered it. The whole system was perfect for ambushes and traps. In 1868, it was home to many Comanche and Kiowa. After the end of the Civil War, the army was set on driving the Indians from Texas and New Mexico into reservations. To this end, they attacked their villages and harried them until a large body of Comanche and Kiowa retreated into Palo Duro and set up villages there. From this secure location they could go on the warpath, raid nearby areas and then scuttle back to the canyons, where nobody durst follow them. In addition to the Comanche and Kiowa, Palo Duro also gave temporary shelter to various bands of Comancheros. The army did not enter the canyons, because they were a deathtrap. The men holed up there knew every inch of the place and could snipe from clifftops, sally forth unex-pectedly and generally lead regular soldiers a merry dance. Attacking Indian villages out on the plains was one thing; guerrilla warfare in the canyons quite another.

The Comancheros were traders from New Mexico, mainly Spanish or half-breed, who supplied the Indians with goods on an exchange or barter basis. They might swap flour, cloth, tools and tobacco for hides or livestock. Some of the Comancheros were just regular business people, travelling salesmen whose customers happened to live in Indian villages instead of in towns or on farms. Others, though, had more profitable dealings with the Indians. Once the US Army was engaged in more-or-less open war with them, the Comanche and Kiowa stopped even pretending to follow the white man's ways and fell back into their old life, which consisted mainly of raiding their neighbours and stealing their horses and livestock. This paid better, when trading with the Comancheros, than just hides. Increasingly that year, what the Comanche wanted in return from the Comancheros was not tobacco or cloth, but guns and powder. The last thing the

Comancheros wanted was to see their trading partners driven out of the region and so they had what you might term a vested interest in helping the Indians resist the army. They did this by running guns into the district, often right under the nose of the army.

The Indians found that an even more valuable commodity to trade with, paying higher returns than either livestock or hides, was white captives. The white men usually fought to the death in defence of their families, leaving only the women and children to be captured. Women and children acquired in this fashion by the Comanche and Kiowa were of no real use to them, but certain groups of Comancheros were keen to buy them. Some of these captives could be ransomed by their family or friends, while others could be smuggled into Mexico where they would be used in brothels. There was a high premium on pretty young girls who were still virgins. This trade amounted, in all but name, to slavery.

With General Sheridan rampaging around Texas with his troops and doing his best to round up the Indians on the one side, and Comanche and Kiowa on the other side, raiding farms and waylaying travellers, and with the Comancheros helping to stir things up from purely commercial motives, things were pretty lively round that part of Texas in the summer of 1868. Pastor Faulkner could hardly have chosen a worse time to go up against a gang of ruthless bandits who were prepared to trade young girls in exchange for powder and guns.

Jonas Faulkner felt terrible when he woke up the following morning. He was stiff as a board and had a pain in his hip from lying on a stone. The best thing he felt he could do was to get moving as soon as possible. Ten or fifteen miles from the start of the Palo Duro Canyons was a little town called Santa Pueblo. He had not been there for a year or so, the place being outside his regular circuit, but the pastor seemed to recollect that there was a saloon, a couple of lodging houses, a blacksmith and so on there. It would probably make a good start for his investigations. At the very least, he might hear news of the current situation. Unless he missed his guess, in which case it would have been a few miles outside that town that the girls from the orphanage were seized.

It was a beautiful September morning and Faulkner was wishing that his journey was not one likely to end in violence. He was trotting along the road and the sky was that deep cerulean blue that you see at that time of year. Overhead, a kestrel circled and a jackrabbit hopped out of his path. Everywhere he looked, he could see evidence of God's mercies and here was he, packing a pistol and a Bowie knife and heading off for what looked certain-sure to be a bloody confrontation. Well, he thought, that is how the world is sometimes. It cannot be helped.

It took him the best part of the day to reach Santa Pueblo and when he arrived, it was just as he remembered it, excepting that there looked to be more money about than when last he had been there. Quite a few of the passers-by in the street were olive-skinned men of Spanish origin and it did not take much working out to conclude that the Comancheros used this place as some kind of staging post. Faulkner was glad of the impulse that had brought him here and felt sure that somebody in the saloon that evening would be able to set him on the right path. It was late afternoon and the long ride had not done Faulkner's posterior any good. It was some years since he had ridden hard like this from sunup to getting on towards dusk. He had a misery in his back, too, which almost doubled him up in pain once he had dismounted.

His memory had not played him false and he found one or two houses letting rooms by the night; one of them being run by a little widow-woman who seemed honoured to have a minister staying at her place. After making provision for Jenny at the livery stable, Faulkner washed and freshened up in a decent, if sparsely furnished, little room. He concealed his pistol and knife under the mattress. He did not aim to be engaging in any gun-play here, at any rate. His room was on the ground floor and he opened the window to smell the evening air.

Mrs McKenzie, the lady who owned the house, was as talkative as Faulkner could have hoped, confirming what he had suspected: that Santa Peublo was undergoing a little boom, with plenty of money floating around that year.

'To what do you attribute this prosperity, Mrs McKenzie?' Faulkner asked, while eating a light supper, which the widow had been kind enough to rustle up for him.

'Why, I guess it's down to the Coman-cheros. They have plenty of cash money to spend and are pretty free with it. Mind, I don't inquire where they get it.'

'They buy and sell from the Indians, don't they?' said Faulkner innocently.

'Yes, but what are they selling? That's the question.'

'Coffee?' hazarded Pastor Faulkner. 'Flour, maybe?'

Mrs McKenzie leaned towards him and lowered her voice. 'Guns!'

'No, really?' asked Faulkner, doing his best to appear shocked by this intelligence. 'Why would they do that?'

'General Sheridan has orders to round up all the Indians and move them onto a reservation. They won't go. Since the army came here there's been nothing but trouble with the redskins, I can tell you.'

'Didn't I hear something about some young girls being snatched near here?'

'Terrible, terrible. The Indians took them and everybody says that they are being kept prisoner in Palo Duro. They say that one of these days, the army is going to go in there and clear them all out. I fear that it will be too late for those poor children by then, though.'

Once it was dark and he had eaten, Faulkner told Mrs McKenzie that he was going for a good long walk and headed to the outskirts of town. Then he doubled back on his tracks and went to the saloon. It put him rather in mind of the cantinas of Mexico in which he had drunk as a young man. It certainly wasn't anything like a usual saloon in any normal town. For one thing, nearly all those drinking there looked to be of either Spanish or Indian origin. There were only a handful of white Anglos. He felt mighty conspicuous in his long, heavy black coat. I have 'preacher' written all over me, thought Faulkner to himself. It will be a regular miracle if I can get anybody in this place to open up and provide me with information. He went to the bar and ordered a glass of juice from the young girl serving there. She looked dubious, but returned after some delay with a sharp-tasting liquid which defied Pastor Faulkner's palate to identify what fruit it might have come from.

Faulkner turned round to survey the room a little closer. A group of swarthy-looking types were playing cards at one table and various other parties were discussing business in low tones. It did not strike him as a place full of men relaxing; more a collection of business meetings. Nearly everybody present was packing a pistol or two and he wondered if his appearing here without one was something in the nature of a breach of etiquette. The more narrowly he observed the scene in front of him, the more did he become convinced that his initial guess was correct and that this little town was at the crossroads of the Comanchero trade between Palo Duro and New Mexico. Establishing this in his mind, though, took him no further forward in his efforts to track down the men who currently held the girls from the Oneida Orphans' Asylum. He turned to the girl behind the bar, saying, 'I mind that many of the men here are traders and suchlike. Would I be right in thinking that some are now based in the canyons up at Palo Duro?'

It seemed to Faulkner that an innocent question of this sort would come quite naturally from somebody like him, looking like what he was — an elderly church minister. Nobody would be likely to take it as anything other than a casual inquiry by a man who knew no better than to talk about such matters. The effect on the young girl, though, was remarkable. Her eyes widened in fear and she asked in a low voice, 'Why are you asking me about that? I don't know nothing.'

'Just making conversation. No harm meant, I'm sure.'

'Leave me be, I don't know about any traders.'

It was pretty clear to Pastor Faulkner that he had struck gold with his first attempt and he decided to back off now and then pursue the girl later, when there were fewer people round. Cross-questioning her right now in a cantina full of rough-looking Comancheros was not the smart move. The girl looked scared and Faulkner was about to turn and leave it for the moment when he felt a sharp jab in his back. He ignored it and was rewarded by another, harder shove.

'What you been saying to the lady to frighten her?'

Faulkner turned round to face the person who had spoken. It was a young fellow, about twenty or so, with a fresh and open face. He was staring at Faulkner with dislike. 'Old gentleman like you, preacher, too, if I'm not mistook, pestering a lady in that way. I call it disgusting.'

The young man's companion, who looked to be much the same age but a mite meaner, repeated, 'Disgusting.'

'Listen, boys, I'm thinking that there has been some species of misunderstanding here. I am not bothering this young lady and if I have upset her, then I apologize, both to her and to the two of you.' This was so fair spoken and humble that Faulkner made sure that it would be enough to end the awkwardness, but the two boys had been drinking heavily and were spoiling for a fight.

The one who had prodded him in the back and first spoken gave him a shove in the chest, saying, 'Well, it ain't what I would call good enough, see?'

Giving an inward sigh, the Reverend Faulkner decided that if his mission was not to be jeopardized, he would have to stop this from developing any further. Both young men were carrying pistols in ordinary holsters. He held out his hands, palms outwards in a placating gesture. 'I'm not looking for any trouble,' he said. Then he whipped both hands up and brought them hard against the sides of the two boys' heads, banging their skulls together with enough force to make a sharp crack, which echoed through the cantina, bringing conversation to a halt and drawing all eyes to the situation at the bar. Before the men in front of him had realized what had happened, Faulkner reached down and plucked their pistols from the holsters, cocking and pointing both guns at them. 'I'm not looking for any trouble,' he said again, 'but if you boys are looking for trouble, I've got plenty and to spare.'

The dazed young men stared stupidly at the levelled revolvers, wondering how they had come to be buffaloed by a man who looked to be old enough to be their grandfather. Faulkner stared back at them, expressionless. 'I wasn't bothering this young lady. I just asked her a question about this area, I'm new in town. Now, are we going to fall out or would you fellows like to shake hands and then part our ways without any hard feelings?'

The crack on the head had apparently done the boys some good or at the very least sobered them up some. They did not appear to be nearly so keen on starting a fight now. Mind, the fact that they were looking down the barrels of a couple of .45s might have had what you could describe as a calming effect upon their passions.

All eyes in the cantina were now upon the little drama being played out by the bar. Even the poker players had stopped their game to watch, with interest, what would happen next. Faulkner had the idea that it was probably not uncommon for violence to erupt like this in the place. The young men made no move, either to speak or act. They did not look like bad characters and on an impulse, the preacher gave a quick flick of the two guns, which caused the boys to flinch in fear and provoked sharp intakes of breath from some of the other men in the smoky room. He had simply reversed the weapons, so that he was now holding the barrels, offering the hilts towards the men to whom they belonged.

'Go ahead, take them. I think that there has been some kind of misunderstanding. I am sorry for giving you sore heads, but you were being mighty provoking. I was not bothering this young woman, as I am sure she will agree.' Pastor Faulkner glanced at the girl, who gave a scared but emphatic nod. The two young men took hold of their pistols. 'You fellows ain't about to shoot me in the back, I suppose?' Saying which, he turned on his heel and walked slowly out of the bar.

He got a dozen paces down the dark street, when one of the two men he had disputed with called out, 'Hey, Preacher!' He and his friend had both followed Faulkner.

He turned warily to face them. 'Well, boys, I am at your mercy. You had best make your move; I am unarmed.' He twitched his coat aside to show them that he was not carrying.

'Hell, Preacher, we ain't going to shoot you. We come out to say sorry. Got a bit carried away, like. Marie said you were just asking about those Comancheros who hang out here. Shake?'

Pastor Faulkner walked to the men and reached out his hand. 'Sorry about striking you both. I felt I had need, but I am sorry all the same.'

'Don't be worrying about that. Me and my partner have had worse than that before now, although never from a man of God. Reckon we misjudged you.'

'Happen you did at that. Goodnight, boys.'

'Night, Preacher.'

The minister gave a sigh of relief as he walked back to the boarding house. He had managed not to get shot and he felt sure that that girl Marie would be able to give him a lead on the children being held up at Palo Duro. It wasn't a bad beginning.

Pastor Faulkner followed his usual nightly ritual of reading the Bible for half an hour or so. When he checked his watch, he found that he had over run his time and that he had been immersed in the Good Book for over an hour. He closed the Bible and went over and opened the window. It was a beautiful night and Jonas Faulkner felt very close to the Lord as he gazed out into the velvety darkness. Overhead, the stars were like a sprinkling of diamond dust, slightly dimmed by the bright yellow moon, which lacked only a day or two until it reached its fullest extent. The sight of it reminded him that it was vital to recover those children before the full moon.

Out in the darkness he heard a soft hiss; somebody was trying to draw his attention. 'Who's there?' he asked in a low voice. The girl from the saloon emerged from the shadows.

'It's Marie, isn't it? What can I do for you?'

'You wanted to know about those men up in the canyons. If you go now to the back of the blacksmith's, somebody there will tell you more about this. I dare not say more.' She faded back into the darkness, leaving the pastor rubbing his chin thoughtfully.

'That scared young creature is acting under duress, or my name's not Jonas Faulkner,' said the preacher to himself. 'What will it be: a bunch of men jumping me and then giving me a beating to warn me off my questioning? Something worse: just one man with a knife, perhaps? We shall see.' He closed the window and dimmed the lamp; there was no point in making a target of himself for anybody outside. Then he reached under the mattress and pulled out the pistol. 'There's trouble in the wind, Jonas, you can bet on it,' he said out loud. He checked the caps and spun the cylinder. 'What did that Oliver Cromwell say? 'Trust to God and keep your powder dry'? I reckon that's about the strength of the case here.' He tucked the pistol in his belt.

Most folks were in bed and those he did pass seemed to be set upon their own business and paid him no heed. The blacksmith's place was all shut up and dark. It did not look as though he lived over the shop. The minister walked up to the building and then edged quietly round to the back, staying pressed right against the wall. No point in giving anybody a silhouette to fire at, if that was the game.

The moonlight showed an empty yard, surrounded on three sides with barns and sheds. The hairs on the back of his neck were prickling; Faulkner just knew that some mischief was afoot. His back still ached a little from sleeping out the previous night. I am getting too old for this sort of game and that is a fact, he thought. He bent down to ease the pain in his back and at that self same moment there was the crack of a rifle and a bullet smacked into the wooden wall of the blacksmith's shop. A fraction of a second earlier and it would have hit him right in his chest. The preacher's response was automatic and deadly. He had already caught a glimpse of a flash from high up on his left and he pulled the pistol from where it was tucked in his pants and drew down in that general direction, spotting the outline of the man on the upper floor of the barn leaning out to take another shot. He fired once and the rifleman gave a cry.

In the silence that followed the shooting, he could hear dogs barking and men calling to each other in the distance. It was time to make tracks. Faulkner was out of condition and he was panting like a sick dog by the time he had sprinted round the back of the buildings on the main street. He was calculating that attention would be focused on the blacksmith's place, but that any inquisitive folk would be waiting a few minutes before they showed themselves round the back. Nobody wants to walk in on a gunfight that does not concern them and folk would wait for a time to make sure that the shooting was over before they investigated. He reached the boarding house safely and managed to open the window to his room from the outside. Once in, he lit the lamp, but kept it turned down low. He threw himself on the bed, without even removing his coat or boots.

The minister lay there for a few minutes, catching his breath back and replaying the scene in his mind, trying to work out whether or not he had killed some man needlessly. He had a special hatred, rooted deep in his outlaw days, for that species of cowardly assassin who lies in wait and shoots a man in the back without warning. As he climbed into bed after saying his prayers, Pastor Faulkner so far forgot his current respectable calling as to mutter something under his breath, which sounded very much like, 'That son of a bitch had it coming to him, anyways.'

3

The next morning, over the breakfast table, Mrs McKenzie was full of news of the shooting by the blacksmith's shop. 'Dead, Reverend Faulkner,' she said breathlessly. 'Shot down and killed behind the blacksmith's. Can you believe it?'

'There is a deal of wickedness in the world, ma'am,' he told her gravely, 'a deal of wickedness.' This was a true enough statement and did not trouble the pastor's conscience from the point of view of telling lies. After all, there surely was a deal of wickedness in the world!

'They say it was some of those Comancheros falling out with each other. Maybe some quarrel over a woman,' said Mrs McKenzie primly. At that moment there was a knock on the door and when she opened it, the lodging-house keeper found standing right there on her doorstep just exactly the sort of woman you might expect Comancheros to be quarrelling about and killing each other over. It was none other than Marie, the girl whose acquaintance Faulkner had made the previous night.

Mrs McKenzie pursed her lips disapprovingly when the young woman asked to see the 'Reverend gentleman'. 'It's all right ma'am,' said Faulkner, 'I think that this young person is seeking my advice about the future course that her life should be taking. Is that not so, my child?'

Marie looked a little confused. 'I guess.'

'Come, we will take a walk up and down Main Street and I shall endeavour to counsel you about your prospects.'

After he had fetched his coat and left Mrs McKenzie almost expiring from avid curiosity, having declined her offer of consulting with the saloon girl right there in her parlour, the pastor walked with Marie along the street. He observed that she was shaken and her face white, as though she had not slept the previous night.

'I swear to you, Father, I had no idea what that scoundrel purposed last night. He told me that you were some type of investigator tricked out as a parson and he wanted to know what your game was.'

'You've no occasion to call me 'Father'; I'm a Presbyterian, not a Catholic. How come you're not afeared to be seen walking in the streets with me today? I'm guessing that some of those fellows had some sort of hold over you?'

Marie turned and eyed him keenly. 'Yes, that is so. Or at least, it was so, but it was really just the one, him as was killed. He had enough to get me hung if he cared to open his mouth. But you know what, Preacher? He's dead now and so I'm my own woman again. Say, did you shoot him? I guessed you must have, you meeting him there last night and then him getting killed. Was it you?'

'That's nothing to the purpose. What did you come by the lodging house for?'

'To answer the questions that you were asking last night. I reckon I owe you. What do you want to know?'

Reverend Faulkner stopped dead in his tracks and turned to look at the young girl beside him. He could not make up his mind whether or not this was another trick and that she had it in mind to lead him into danger again. Still and all, he didn't rightly see that he had much choice in the matter. It was no manner of use for him to go blundering off into Palo Duro blind, without comprehending what he was up against.

'What is it that you would tell me? I am seeking the whereabouts of six girls and two grown women who were seized by some Kiowa and then sold to a band of Comancheros. Can you set me on their trail? If so, then you would be doing a good piece of work, which might be offset by the Lord against whatever evil you have in the past been mixed up in.'

'I don't know nothing about the Lord. You saved me from being blackmailed for the rest of my life and I am glad of it. I owe you. I will pay the debt. Yes, I know the business of which you speak and can lead you to the hideout where those children are being held.'

'That will not be needful. Only set me on the right track. Give me the directions to the place and I will ride alone. I would not wish to cast you into hazard.'

The woman snorted. 'I been cast into hazard often enough. Don't set mind to that. I am not one for writing or nothing. It is no good expecting me to draw you a map or nothing of that sort. I can lead you there. If you don't want that, then we can forget the entire thing.'

'So be it. Have you a horse?'

'Got a pony; that's enough for a little thing like me.'

'I do not see that there is any percentage in advertising our association. This would not be to my advantage or yours, either, likely enough. I will guess that the road west from here is the beginning of the way. Is that so?'

'I like the way you talk. Are you really a preacher?'

'I am that.'

'Say we team up in two hours, about a mile west of here on that track?'

'That would do admirably. I shall look forward to it.'

'See you in a spell, then.'

Before he went back to Mrs McKenzie's place to pick up his things and settle his bill, Pastor Faulkner decided to pay a visit to the store and see if they had anything that might be useful to him on his expedition.

The store was a gloomy and ill-lit room in a rickety wooden building, just along the way from the livery stable. There were the usual things like large cans of lamp oil, glass chimneys, pots, pans, spades, bolts of cloth and so on,

53

as well as a glass-fronted case containing an assortment of firearms. The proprietor came out of the back and greeted Faulkner amiably. 'Not often we get a man of the cloth in here, Padre. Looking for anything special?'

'I am wondering if you happen to have such a thing as a muff pistol? I mean a derringer or some such.'

'Sure we have, right here, look. Little .41-calibre numbers, perfect for the ladies.' He took one out of the cabinet to show Faulkner. 'Anything else?'

'Do you sell black powder?'

'Yes, sir, I got some right out the back.'

'You have fuses, too?'

The shopkeeper was looking at the preacher like he was some rare freak of nature. 'Reverend, you don't mind me asking, is all this for you?'

'It is.'

'You ain't aiming to pass any of it on to a minor?'

'Why would I do that?'

'I have to ask, it's the law.'

'No, it's for my own use. You want me to sign your book for the pistol?'

The shopkeeper passed the register over to Pastor Faulkner, and pushed an inkwell and pen towards him. 'You want any ammunition for the derringer?'

'Yes, let me have a box of .41 rimfire if you have them, please.'

'How much powder you want?'

'Tell me, do you have a five-pound keg?'

'That we do.'

After Faulkner had made his purchases and left the store, the owner went out and stared after him as he walked back to Mrs McKenzie's house. 'That surely is the strangest preacher that I have come across in a good, long time,' he said to himself.

A small child was hurrying down the street, carrying an open pitcher in her hand. She could not have been more than seven or eight and Jonas Faulkner shook his head disapprovingly at the sight of such a little thing being sent to run errands instead of sitting in a schoolroom. As the little girl trotted past an elegantly dressed, middle-aged, swarthy-looking man, she stumbled slightly and a stray splash from the jug shot up and left a few spots on the man's cream-coloured breeches.

'Why, you little . . . ' the fellow said and lifted his hand to take a swipe at the scared child, who was already stuttering an apology. Before he could bring his hand down on the girl's head, his wrist was suddenly clamped fast in what felt like an immovable vice. He struggled to free his arm and then turned in amazement to see who had had the unspeakable temerity to lay hands on the person of Alfonso Rodriquez y Trevisa y Gonsalez.

Before releasing the stranger's wrist, Faulkner told the child, 'You run along now, little britches. I saw what happened; it was a pure accident. Don't be afeared.' The little girl stared at him for a second and then went swiftly on her way. Pastor Faulkner turned to the man whose arm he had a hold of. 'As for you, my friend, you need to be a little more careful about striking children. I could, if I had the time, show you the relevant passages in scripture, but I am guessing that you are a Catholic and perhaps know of them already. Set a watch upon that temper of yours, or it will lead you astray some day.' He let go of the man's arm and made to move off.

'Wait,' said the man. Faulkner turned back. 'You are right. I have had a bad day and should not have behaved as I did. You are a man of God?'

'I am.'

'You love children also, I think?'

Faulkner said nothing, but looked at the man, trying to gauge his intentions.

'I think I saw you in the cantina last night,' said the well-dressed man. I was astonished to see you deal so neatly with those two hot-headed boys. You did not act then as I think many priests would have been able to do. What is your name?'

'Faulkner. Jonas Faulkner.'

The man stretched out his hand. 'Well, Mr Faulkner, or should I say Reverend Faulkner? You are really a priest? Will you shake my hand?' They shook and Faulkner touched his hat brim to the fellow before stalking off to the lodging house. The Spanish-looking man, who was actually Portuguese, gazed after him thoughtfully.

Mrs McKenzie was just itching to find out the nature of Faulkner's business with Marie. Something about her put the minister strongly in mind of Mrs O'Hara. She had the same rare gift for cross-examining a man mercilessly under the pretext of an elderly widow's artless chatter.

'That young woman, now. I would have taken oath that she was not the sort to be seeking out a parson. But perhaps I measured her character wrong?' Pastor Faulkner made an indistinct and non-committal noise in his throat that could have been taken equally well as assent or protest. 'I see you have been to the store. You should have let me go for you. I am there regular as clockwork each day. What would you have in that wooden keg, now, Reverend Faulkner? It wouldn't be brandy, would it?' She dimpled engagingly to indicate to Faulkner that she had been joking.

'It is not brandy, ma'am. I'm a temperance man and have been these many years. Strong drink makes weak men, as they say.'

'Amen to that. I never touch a drop, 'cept for medicinal purposes, of course.'

'I have not the least doubt of it, ma'am. I would not bring intoxicating liquor into a respectable house; you may make sure of that.'

'That girl, now. Marie, is it? Would she be stopping to work in a saloon after you have counselled her? That would be a mercy!'

'It would be, Mrs McKenzie, but even the Devil does not know what lies in a man or woman's heart. We can but hope, ma'am, we can but hope.'

'Will you be staying tonight, Pastor? I

have a piece of lamb in that would do you a power of good. You look to be like a man who does not take care of his body enough.'

'Alas, ma'am, I must be leaving this very day in half an hour or so. Would it be putting you out if I were to ask you to prepare me some cold meat, cheese and a loaf of bread? I shall, of course, expect the reckoning of it to be added to my bill, which I shall settle this minute if it is agreeable to you?'

While the good widow was fluttering about, preparing what she described as a 'picnic' for him and calculating how much she could gouge him for, Faulkner went to his room to prepare for the next stage of his journey. He opened the keg of powder and poured a little into his palm. It was fine-grained and pitch black. He smelt it and then rolled a few grains between his finger and thumb. 'Well, Jonas, you can never carry too much powder with you and that's a fact. You never know when a pound or two of black powder is apt to be just what you need.' In his younger days he had been in the habit of carrying a few pounds of black powder in his saddlebag, the way another man might keep tobacco.

He stripped down his pistol and emptied out the powder that he had charged it with before setting out from Claremont. True, it had fired well enough last night, but it would do no harm to use some fresh powder. The stuff from his attic had been mouldering away up there for over a decade. After a drop of oil, he loaded the Colt with the new powder and then emptied the old charges out the window into the flowerbed. He then loaded the little muff gun, which was not a genuine derringer but one of the many cheap imitations, and tucked it in his boot.

The widow McKenzie watched him craftily as he read the bill, which she presented for one night's lodging, two meals, a few ounces of bacon and cheese and half a loaf of yesterday's bread. She was overcharging him, but not by as much as he had thought she might. Why, he wondered, are people so ready to cheat a clergyman? He was sure that Mrs McKenzie would not have inflated her bill so readily had he been a travelling salesman.

After he and the good widow had sworn undying friendship for each other and he had promised to stay there the very next time he should happen to find himself in Santa Pueblo, the preacher managed to tear himself away and get off to the livery stable to pick up his horse. I wonder by how much that fellow will think he can rob a poor old parson, thought Faulkner gloomily, as he strode down Main Street. A couple of dark-skinned men touched their hats to him as he passed. He had an idea that his dispute with the two boys the previous night had been witnessed and widely discussed in the town. It struck him that by the time he came back here, the widow McKenzie would also be likely to have heard the story. That might change her view of me entirely, he thought.

After he had been duly cheated by the owner of the livery stable, although to a somewhat lesser degree than had been the case with the lodging-house landlady, he made off out of town at a slow trot, being somewhat ahead of his time.

It had been a dry, hot summer and the road was dusty. Still and all, it was a pleasant enough journey. Although he had no clear idea of how to go about the job, it seemed to Pastor Faulkner that if the girl from the saloon could only lead up as far as the Comanchero camp, then he would have to trust in the Lord and, as the saying goes, play it by ear. He had one advantage, which he had not so far mentioned to anybody, and that was that he had ridden with the Comancheros as a young man. He knew a good deal about their ways and also spoke a little of the strange slang that they used among themselves. It wasn't much, but at least it was some sort of edge.

Marie was already waiting for Faulkner about a mile out of town. She was wearing pants instead of a skirt and looked somewhat of a tomboy. 'I should not have recognized you,' he told her, 'had we not met by arrangement. You are a different person in that getup. Cleaner and healthier, I should say. Well, will you lead on?'

'What will you do if I take you to the base? You are not a man of violence?'

'I am a man of God. I shall ask them to surrender up those children and their teachers. If they do so peaceably, there will be no call for bloodshed.'

'Surrender up peaceably? Reverend, do you know what sort of men these are?'

'Yes. I have no illusions about that. Nevertheless, I shall ask first. If they then wish to set to with me, then we shall see what we see.'

The girl looked at him curiously. 'You know, you're not like any preacher I ever set eyes upon. Ain't you afeared of what might befall you?'

'Not overmuch. If they let me take those people back with me, then we shall part on what you might describe as amiable terms.'

'You are one crazed man!' she shrugged. 'Well, Preacher, it's your funeral. I'll lead you there and then I'm back for town.'

The Reverend Faulkner was staring back along the way he had come. His eyes narrowed as he saw wisps of dust a mile or two off. He turned to the girl. 'You wouldn't play me false, would you, child?'

'No, but happen I have not told you the full story.'

'That's like enough to be true. Well, what's the game?'

'There are two more men riding with us to Palo Duro. They have some business of their own there and I offered to act as guide for them, too.'

'They paying you?'

'Not exactly.'

The minister reached behind him and drew his pistol from the saddle roll, tucking it into his belt where it was handy. Marie watched with a look of alarm on her face. 'You ain't about to shoot them, Reverend, are you?'

'Not a bit of it. I just want to be ready for any trouble.' It came as no special surprise to Jonas Faulkner when the men drew near enough to be identified and he saw that it was the two young men that he had buffaloed the night before. They smiled cheerfully when they reached the minister and saloon girl.

'Hidy!' said the more pleasant-looking of the two boys to Faulkner. The preacher responded by plucking the revolver from his belt, cocking it and drawing down on them. 'Shit, Reverend, there's no call for that!'

'Suppose you boys tell me the play?'

'Nothing, sir. Marie here says that you want to find those girls being held up at Palo Duro. We have some business up that way ourselves and so we thought we'd throw in with you. Old gentleman like you, you might be glad

66

of a little protection.'

Faulkner stared at them for a moment or two and then put the pistol back in his belt. 'You boys on the scout?'

'I couldn't say no and I couldn't say yes, either. It is by way of being a long story.'

'I'll be bound it is,' said Faulkner. 'Well, I seemingly have little choice in the matter. Let's ride on.'

The two boys tried to engage the preacher in light conversation about where he lived and how he came to be going to Palo Duro and so on, but finding that he was not disposed to chat idly they fell to talking between themselves and sometimes drawing the girl into their chatter. They seemed pleasant enough young fellows, but it was plain as a pikestaff to Faulkner that they were up to some sort of mischief. He could not exactly figure out what it might be, but at a guess he would have said that it was something in the thieving, rather than murdering, line.

The ill-assorted party rode on until the early afternoon, when Marie called a halt. They had ridden south for a space and then turned east onto a barely defined dust track. It was arid, dry country; not precisely desert, but certainly not fertile or arable land, either. If this little adventure lasted more than a couple of days, then they would be going hungry, thought Faulkner. Living off the land did not look to be a practical proposition and the chances of coming across a boarding house or saloon to supply their needs out here in the wilderness were slender. Mind, presumably the Kiowa and Comanche managed to find enough to eat and drink out here.

'Listen, now,' said Marie, 'we have to stop here until nightfall. We must set up camp out of sight. This track is used by people regular, and we have been lucky not to have come across anybody yet. We must not push our chances.'

'What happens when it gets dark?' asked Faulkner.

'We enter the canyon,' said Marie. 'You can see ahead where Palo Duro begins. From the start of it, it is maybe eight or ten miles to the place where those children are being kept.'

The minister turned round in his saddle to address the two young men. 'Either of you boys been in Palo Duro before?'

'No, Reverend, Marie has not yet led any of us there.'

'Come on,' said the girl, 'if we stay here much longer, somebody will come by and see us.' She set off at a canter towards a formation of rocks half a mile or so from the track. The three men followed on.

The worn, reddish rocks, some of which were the size of small houses, provided a good place to make a temporary camp while they waited for it to get dark. The four of them pooled their food and made a fairly decent picnic meal. The only thing lacking was a pot of coffee to finish with, but it didn't rightly seem like the smart dodge to start up a fire so close to the trail into Palo Duro. The two younger men satisfied themselves with rolling cigarettes and then leaning back and relaxing. After they had all been reclining so for ten minutes or thereabouts, one of the boys spoke to Faulkner.

'Say, Preacher, how come you are so ready to use a pistol when the going gets rough? Is it true what Marie here tells us, that you shot that Comanchero who was putting the bite on her?'

Pastor Faulkner stared gloomily into the clear blue sky. 'It's true enough. You boys could do a sight worse than take a warning from my life. I know where carrying on the way you two are leads a man. You are decent enough rogues today, but the path leads downwards and who knows where it will take you? Ten years from now you may be given over to all sorts of beastliness.'

'Well,' said one of the men, 'I reckon you might know more about that than us. Why not tell us about your own life? How comes it that a man like you, who

I would say knows a thing or two himself about the world, ended up in the preaching line of work?'

Faulkner brooded for a moment or two and then replied, 'You speak truly. Mayhap it might do you fellows some good to hear how the trail you are now on might lead you to worse things than you could ever dream of. I shall tell you how it came that I am now a man of God, and you shall judge for your own selves if or not you should turn aside from the lives you are living.' He thought for a moment and then began to talk of his early life. The other three listened, captivated by the strange tale he told them.

4

'I do not know why I should have turned out as I did. My mother and father were God-fearing folks and I was certainly raised right. It says in the Good Book, 'Raise up a child in the way he should go and he will not depart from it even in old age,' but that is not always the case; not by a long chalk. Well, that's nothing to the purpose. Fact is, by the time I was eighteen, I was on the scout with a crew of regular villains. We did not generally kill people, because there was no percentage in it. Had it been to our advantage, though, I make no doubt that we would have shot down many innocent persons.

'As it was, those we did kill were usually other thieves and low types. There were squabbles over the division of our spoils, arguments about women and pointless disputes with complete strangers in saloons. I reckon that I myself must have shot something like thirty men, half of whom proceeded to die from their wounds. Imagine that; I killed so many men that I am unable to keep an accurate tally. Mind, that was because for a good deal of that time, I was in liquor. I drank heavy as any man could for the best part of twenty years and I was always at my meanest when I was in my cups or 'liquored up', as you boys would probably call it.

'Now, me and the sort of boys I rode with, we would plot most any scheme that would be like to bring us in money. We robbed stages, held up folk in their own homes, knocked over banks and undertook practically anything else that might pay. There was no crime too low for us at that time and we each of us had a good price on our heads.

I maintained this dreadful life for twenty years, interspersing my robberies with work in saloons, running crooked card games and even working as a lawman for a while. By the time I was coming up to my fortieth birthday, I was as hardened a wretch as you could ever meet. I had picked up with a set of younger men, men who would stop at nothing. They would josh me a little, calling me 'old-timer' and so on, because I was old enough to be their father. They would also make the odd joke about how I was more cautious than them, stopping short of accusing me of cowardice, though, because they knew that I would shoot anybody who even hinted at such a thing.

'Well, we ended up one time, the four of us, in a small town near to some mountains. It doesn't signify exactly where. It was a nice little town and a road ran through it, which connected to larger towns. We fetched up there and spent a few days playing cards and wondering what particular piece of villainy we should get up to next, as we were running out of money. One of our party heard somehow that a stage that was soon due in town was carrying money from one bank to another. The bank generally provided an armed guard to ride shotgun on such transfers of funds and they were tempting targets to people such as me and my friends.

'The afternoon that we heard this rumour, we four rode out of town to look out the route that the stage would take when it left the town where we were staying. The road wound up into the hills and then twisted through a mountain pass. There, the road was surrounded by rocky outcrops and made a sudden turn before crossing a rickety wooden trestle bridge, which crossed a little river. It was not a high bridge: it ran perhaps forty feet above the river. The road it carried consisted of lengths of timber like railroad sleepers.

'Now, you could not see this bridge as you were approaching it, because of the cliffs and rocky slopes. The road took a sudden sharp turn to the left, so that one would have to slow a horse and cart or stagecoach right down. There was a big sign at this point, warning travellers to take care ahead of them, because there was a narrow bridge. The bridge itself was that narrow that only one vehicle at a time could cross. We figured that this would be the ideal place for an ambush. If we jumped the stage there, as they had stopped to read the warning sign, we could steal the money, cut the traces on the stage or shoot the horses and then make off over the bridge to escape. It all seemed just so easy.

'Right on time the next day, the stage arrived and proceeded to change horses and give passengers the chance to stretch their legs, answer calls of nature and so on. The bank guard looked to be a fairly capable young fellow and if anybody would be giving us trouble it was he. He was sitting perched up next to the driver, with a carbine cradled in his arms. The passengers were two elderly ladies, a respectable-looking man and a mother and her child. It would be a question of making sure that the driver and bank guard both knew that we meant business. The passengers could be left out of the reckoning.

'We boys rode up into the hills and prepared ourselves for action. We looked like a bunch of desperados, with handkerchiefs tied over our mouths and all the rest of it. The stage came up the road and, just as we had calculated, it stopped at the big sign so that the driver could read it and see what preparations he should make for crossing the bridge, which, as I have remarked, could not even yet be seen from that point. It was then that we rode down to the stage and desired all on board to cast down their weapons and deliver up to us the box containing the bank's money.

'Now, one thing I have noticed time after time in operations of this sort is that those in the same business as us, although on the opposite side, as you might say, tend to follow the rules pretty well. What I mean by this is that bank guards and lawmen will generally make a good decision about when to fight and when to hold fire. This has the effect of making some robberies and arrests almost good-natured affairs, with both sides knowing how to behave. It is like we are all playing the same game, although belonging to opposing teams, if you take my meaning. In this particular instance, the bank guard saw that he was facing four men with drawn weapons and he had no intention of sacrificing his life for the sake of other folks' cash. He threw down his rifle at once and raised his hands.

'So far, everything was proceeding just as sweetly as we could have wished. The only strange thing was that I thought I could hear some singing off in the distance, like the sound of children's voices. I had just begun to wonder what this could be, when the well-dressed and respectable man I had seen boarding the stage earlier in the day leaned out of the window with a revolver in his hand and shot dead the man next to me. He had no occasion to do this, the robbery being none of his affair. Another of my companions opened fire, shooting the man in the stage, and then all hell broke loose, figuratively and, I truly believe, quite literally, too. The driver, fearing that he was about to be caught up in the middle of a gun battle, whipped on his horses and took off. We followed, firing our guns at the stagecoach, feeling that we had been cheated out of our money, to say nothing of seeing a good friend gunned down needlessly.

'The stage picked up speed and took the bend fast, tilting on two wheels, and then came immediately to the little timber bridge that I told you of. By this time, the horses were frantic with terror and quite out of control, what with all the gunfire and so on, and the stage and four horses thundered straight onto the bridge. Coming from the other direction was a wagonload of children, the ones I had heard singing as we tried to hold up the stage. The open wagon was pulled by one horse and the driver had got off to lead the horse over the bridge. There were only low, rickety wooden rails preventing anybody from falling off the side of the bridge and he was just leading the horse on at a slow and steady walk. He and the wagon full of children were halfway across the bridge.

'I may as well tell you now what I read later in the newspapers, and that was that this was a Sunday School outing returning from a picnic up in the hills. There was the old fellow driving the wagon, two lady teachers and eleven children, the oldest but eleven years of age.

'The stage careered along that narrow bridge and I could hardly bear to watch, because it was almost as though I had been vouchsafed a vision of the future and knew just precisely what was about to happen.

'The children were screaming and I saw the two women reaching out in a vain attempt to gather up those helpless little ones and shepherd them to safety.

There was no time, of course, because the next second, that stage and four horses smashed into the wagon, over-turning it entirely and tipping the children and their Sunday School teachers forty feet into the dried-up river-bed below. Even then, some of them might have survived — they were lying there injured and screaming for a second — but next thing, the horses of the stage had carried on with their headlong rush and the wagon had broken through the wooden railings and fallen off the bridge, taking the horse with it. These two heavy items fell on top of the injured children and as if that were not enough, the lead horses of the stagecoach went over as well. For a fraction of a second the stage was balanced there on the bridge, before it, too, went off the bridge and also landed on the children and their teachers. All the children as had been on that picnic perished that day, as did the two ladies with them, the drivers of the wagon and the stagecoach, the two elderly lady passengers and the child who was also in the stage. The only survivor from the event was the mother, who had been travelling in the stagecoach with her child. She was paralyzed for life, but not killed. Twelve children and six adults died; well, seven adults if you count the passenger who opened fire on us and began the process that ended in that terrible massacre.

'My partners in this foul deed urged on their horses and cried that we should leave at once, but I could not bring myself to do this. Instead, I noticed a little rough track leading down to the river and I set my horse along this, aiming to see if anybody had survived and could be helped. I knew well enough that this was a hanging matter, but even so I could not just ride off and leave the scene. I think that this was when the Lord first spoke clearly to me and I broke off from that broad path that leads to destruction. My comrades were making various observations such as, 'What in the hell is the old-timer up to?' and calling out, 'Come on, man, we best dig up and be out of here!'

'Well, I got down to the creek and made my way over to the splintered wreckage of the stage and the smashed-up bodies of the horses and people. My 'friends' had taken off, realizing, perhaps, that an incident of this sort would be guaranteed to stir the townsfolk up into forming a posse and lynching the perpetrators. I dismounted and was looking helplessly at the slaughter that I had helped to cause, when there was the crack of a rifle and a bullet hit the rocks near me. From reading the newspaper accounts later, this affair becoming what you might term a famous tragedy, I discovered that the bank guard who had surrendered so promptly had jumped off the stagecoach, unseen by us, as it slowed down at the bend, preparatory to crossing the bridge. In all the excitement, we did not see him. He had retrieved his rifle and was now up on the bridge shooting at me.

'It was plain I could do nothing there anyway and so I fired back at him a couple of times, jumped on my horse and rode off up the river-bed, aiming to place as much distance between me and that place as was humanly possible.

'I was cunning as a fox in those days and managed to change direction and use the water to throw any pursuers off the scent. I durst not carry out any more robberies or even so much as spit on the sidewalk, for fear that it would draw attention to me. The hue and cry for the villains who had carried out this massacre extended across the whole state. I had little other choice than to make my way to my father's house, where he took me in and sheltered me. My mother had died a year or two before and I had been so busy with my criminal career that I could not even find the time to attend her funeral. Imagine that, and that my father forgave me without question, took me in and sheltered me. He must himself have been sixty-odd at that time; nigh on the age that I am now myself, which is a sobering reflection.

'My father was a God-fearing man and he gave it as his opinion that the only way of redeeming myself was to dedicate my life to the Lord. I was baptized and after my father exerted some little influence I was admitted to a theological college. He never said a word about the things that I had told him of my life on the scout, saying only that it was between me and my Maker. And so I studied hard and qualified as a minister. I have been at the First Presbyterian Church at Claremont since then and aim to end my days in that place; ministering to the needy and trying to make what amends I am able for the worthless life I led for the first forty years after my birth.

'I tell you boys this story to show what results from the sort of life that I can see you are leading. It starts well enough with excitement, liquor and girls, but believe you me, the end of it is a different matter altogether. If you are not shot in a saloon, you will kick out your life on the end of a rope and if by some good fortune you escape that, then you will grow meaner and more cowardly with each passing year, sinking lower and lower until you end as I did, carrying out the most beastly of crimes.

'Give it up now, while you are still able and have not gone too far. I do not know the nature of your business up in yonder canyon, but I would take oath that it has some reference to robbery. Yes, you do well to smile, but I can see it in your faces.'

5

There was a stunned silence after Reverend Faulkner finished telling his story, a silence which lasted for a minute or so. Then one of the boys said softly, 'That's one hell of a story, Reverend.'

Marie then said, 'Still and all, that was better than fifteen years ago. You cannot go on feeling sorry about the business for ever. It's not like you meant to kill those children, it was by way of being an accident.'

'Some accident,' said Faulkner. 'Suppose now I put on a blindfold and then walk out into the street firing a pistol all over the place. Is the hapless person I shoot dead the victim of an 'accident'? I can tell you now that that would be murder, whether I was aiming at my victim or not. That is the legal position and it is also, I am afraid, what the

Lord himself would say.' He stared moodily into space.

'Do you not think the Lord will make allowance for the circumstances?' asked the other young man.

'A day has not passed since I carried out that terrible act that I do not think long and hard upon those poor children. A day? No, not even an hour has gone by without me thinking on it. As for forgiveness, let me tell you this. On the Day of Judgement, when I stand before the Lord, he will not be throwing his arm round my shoulders and saying, 'Come in, Pastor Jonas, and set yourself down at my table. Sure is good to see you!' No, he will be standing there with his arms around those children I killed and he will say, 'Faulkner, you son of a bitch, why did you slaughter these little ones?''

Faulkner's tale had put somewhat of a dampener on the spirits of the other three people sitting round the fire and there was no more conversation. He moved off a little space and announced that he would take a nap until the sun had set.

When he awoke, as the stars were coming out, Faulkner noticed at once that the woman and one of the men were not in sight. He smiled and guessed that they had crept off behind a rock for some romantic assignation, as it is sometimes called. The other boy had also been sleeping and he woke at that point and asked, 'Where's my partner?'

'You must not ask of me where he and that girl have got to. It is no affair of mine.'

Hearing voices, the two truants emerged, looking a little furtive and casting anxious glances at Faulkner. The boy said, 'Sorry about that, Reverend, but it is what you might term human nature.'

Faulkner laughed. 'There are worse things a man can do than lay with a woman. It is nothing to me.'

After they had all had another bite to eat, Reverend Faulkner decided to lay his hand over and show these young people how things stood. 'I have enjoyed visiting with you young folk and you have made the journey here all the more pleasant for your company, for which I thank you. Howsoever, this is not your business. It is now my intention to go up against some of the most dangerous men you could ever fear to stumble across and I would not wish to lead you all into danger. You must make your ways either forward to the canyon or back to Santa Pueblo as the spirit takes you and I shall proceed alone on my errand.'

One of the young men coughed as though embarrassed. 'The truth is, Preacher, we have not been precisely straight with you.'

'You astonish me, son,' said Faulkner dryly. 'This is a development which I could not have foreseen.'

'You say what?' asked the other boy in bewilderment.

His partner laughed and said, 'The Reverend's joshing with you. He means that he guessed we were up to no good. Ain't that right, Pastor?'

Faulkner nodded good-naturedly. The two men reminded him of his younger self and he was curious to know just what they were about. Something in the thieving line would be his guess. As if he had read the pastor's mind, one of the men shook his head smilingly. 'No, it's not what you think, Reverend. Listen, I'll be straight with you.'

'This is indeed finding Saul among the prophets,' said the minister approvingly. 'I am listening carefully.'

The young fellow turned to his partner and said, 'What do you say I tell it straight to Reverend Faulkner?'

His companion shrugged. 'If you say so.'

'The fact is, Pastor, me and my friend make our money out of claiming rewards.'

Faulkner looked at the young man with undisguised loathing. 'You are bounty hunters?'

'Hell, no! Do we look that type? No,

we hunt down stolen goods and suchlike. Banks and other companies offer rewards for information leading to the recovery of various items. We find out the information, give it to those as are looking and collect the reward.'

Faulkner eyed the two young men warily. If there was one breed of man he could not abide, it was a bounty hunter. 'I suppose next you will be explaining honestly what you are doing following me like this and teaming up on the pretext of taking care of a poor elderly gentleman?'

'It's no complicated matter. Some bullion was stole near here a month ago. We heard where it was taken by a bunch of Comancheros, the same as took those girls you are hunting for. From what we hear, the gold is now held up in their camp somewhere in the Palo Duro Canyon. If we can get a line on it and know when they are moving it, we can tip off the banks and they might be able to seize it back again. If so, we pick up ten per cent, which comes to a right tidy sum.'

There was something so open about the boy's face that Faulkner was convinced. He said slowly, 'So you figured that as I am going to try and recover something from these Comancheros and you are both also interested in something which they hold that we might join forces? Let me rightly understand you: you have done this type of thing before?'

'Sure. Sometimes it comes off and other times not. Anybody with a heap of gold to sell has to take it to a bullion merchant, jewellers or suchlike. Then we call the law, they grab it and we pick up the reward for providing the information. Sometimes we get a reward from the law if they catch the thieves, too.'

Faulkner thought the matter over for a space and then said, 'I will allow that there is some merit in the scheme, but I cannot be a party to it. Those Comancheros would spot two good-natured kids like you a mile off. The result of this foolishness would be the death of you and your friend and this young lady being taken and sold into slavery. I will have no part of it. There is a secondary reason why it does not accord with my plans. This enterprise of mine is like as not to be the death of me as it is. With you children tagging along, it would be a certainty. No, I will act alone.'

'Only, you see, Reverend, that you can't really take that line.' The young man looked as good-humoured as ever, but also stubborn as a jackass.

'Why may I not take this line?' inquired Faulkner.

'Well, you see, Marie here has rather taken to me and I to her. Since she is by way of being the only one of us who knows where those rascally Comancheros are hiding out, it strikes me that she, my partner and I will be making a set with her. If anybody's 'tagging along', as you put it, Reverend, then I guess that's you.'

'What, then, do you propose? That we all work together to the same end?'

'You got it.'

Pastor Faulkner thought the matter over. He liked the boys and Marie seemed a fairly good sort. At length he said, 'Well I guess you have me over a barrel. Very well, let us plan together. I hope you boys are up to some lively tricks and know how to take care of yourselves. My only interest is in those children; I will not risk that mission for the sake of any of you three. You are all three, in a manner of speaking, grown-up people.'

At this moment, they heard the jingling of a harness and realized that a horse was approaching. It was too loud to be on the track into Palo Duro and so a rider had probably left the trail to come and investigate their voices and see who was holed up behind the rocks. Faulkner was up and had his pistol in his hand in a fraction of a second. The other two men were not far behind and so, when an exceedingly swarthy man riding a dappled grey hove into view round the rocks, he found himself facing three tense men with drawn guns.

'Gentlemen, good day to you. I am your servant.'

The minister regarded the man narrowly. It was the same Spanish-looking fellow who he had stopped striking the child earlier that day. Faulkner said, 'We have already met, Mr . . . ?'

'Alfonso Rodriquez y Trevisa y Gonsalez, at your service, sir.' He bowed gracefully, which was no mean feat on horseback.

One of Pastor Faulkner's companions grunted contemptuously. 'Spanish, huh?'

'Portuguese, my dear sir. It is an easy mistake to make, do not reproach yourself.'

'I weren't about to,' muttered the young man.

'May I descend?'

'You go right ahead,' said Faulkner, 'but I should keep your hands in view at all times as you do so and try not to make any sudden moves as might be misinterpreted, if you take my meaning.'

'I apprehend your meaning perfectly, my friend.'

The elegant-looking man dismounted and strolled towards the group, seemingly not in the slightest degree bothered about the three guns, which were still aimed at him. He bowed low to Marie and then sat down on a convenient rock. The others also sat, without holstering their pieces, but no longer actually pointing them at the man who called himself Gonsalez.

Faulkner said, 'Suppose you tell us what you are about, sir, and then we can see how we are to proceed. Your turning up in this way could look a little suspicious to those less open and trusting than the present company. I guess you are on the track of the same bunch of Comancheros as us. What is your interest in them?'

'Beautifully spoken,' said Gonsalez. 'You are right. I make no secret of the matter to you who are 'on the same track', as you say. The truth is, my sister was escorting some children from an orphans' asylum. She was taken by the Indians and is now in the canyons, being held by some Comancheros. I hope to rescue her.' He smiled at everybody in what was evidently meant to be an engaging fashion.

Pastor Faulkner shook his head irritably. 'This whole affair is turning into a three-ring circus,' he growled. 'None of this accords with my plans, which would consist of me alone going against these men. I already have two callow youths and a saloon girl; now a tailor's dummy has joined the party.' He looked disapprovingly at the Portuguese man's fancy clothes.

Gonsalez did not seem in the least bit affronted at being called a tailor's dummy. He turned to the other men and said, 'I am a crack shot. Between the four of us, we should have a better chance than going on one by one. What will you say?'

After a little wrangling, it was fixed that Marie would lead the four of them to the camp, which she said was eight or ten miles away. It was agreed that they would walk, leading their horses, rather than ride, so that the various clanking and chinking that usually signals the approach of a body of mounted men would not give the game away. It was at this point that Faulkner felt that if he really was to be saddled with these companions, he had better instruct them a little in the ways of the Comancheros.

'Listen up, you men. I will have to go ahead of you all a little. The way of it is that there will be at least two sentries as you come to the base. If we just walk up on one of these men, he will start shooting, no question about it. The camp is, at the moment, more or less deserted, apart from the captives and a few men set to guard them.'

'How in the hell do you know that, Preacher? Begging your pardon,' said the more pleasant of the two young men.

'I know it by the moon. The Comanche do most of their raiding by the full moon. It lacks only a day or two until then. Before they go on the warpath, they often have a big feast, lasting a few days. Then, when they have recovered a little, off they set. Have you people never heard of a 'Comanche moon'? It is what they call the full moon in these parts. Any Comancheros around often join in with the party. They will leave a couple of fellows to guard their camp and after a few hours these will be relieved by another couple, the first ones being then able to join the festivities. With luck, the whole crew will be drunk as fiddlers' bitches by now, bar the two or three on guard.'

'You know a lot about this matter, friend,' said the Portuguese man called Gonsalez. 'More than most priests, I am thinking.'

Faulkner said nothing, although everybody was looking towards him and expecting some sort of reply. Eventually, he said, 'There is another thing that you must know. The Comancheros have a kind of language, which they speak among themselves. It is Spanish and Comanche mixed in together with other things. They call it Taibo, which means 'the language'. It is a bit like the Creole that you hear black men using in some places.'

'Padre, why are you delivering this lecture?' asked Gonsalez.

'Because it will save your lives. If we come nigh to the sentry without indicating we are friends, the man is sure to fire on us. Before you know it you'll have every Comanche and Kiowa in the canyons down on us like a duck on a June bug. I can stop this by greeting the sentry in Taibo and persuading him that we are friends. It's nothing to me; you can all take your chances for all I care. My only concern is those children.'

There were a few more words of discussion and it was agreed that Faulkner should go on ahead a-ways when once they were near the Comancheros' camp and that he should parlay with the sentry.

It was almost dark by the time all this

had been settled in a satisfactory manner and they prepared to move out, taking care to muffle anything on the horses that was apt to jingle and thus betray their position in the night. Mind, with the moon that was rising, they would only be hidden from view in narrow, shadowy places. Out in the open, they would be about as visible as if it were the middle of the day.

6

According to Marie, it would take them something like two or three hours to get to the Comancheros' camp if they proceeded at a walk, each leading their horse. As agreed, it was essential for the success of their venture that they should appear without warning. The preacher cross-questioned the girl about what she knew of the place and where he would find the women and girls from the orphanage. It struck him that for a man whose avowed intent was to free his own sister, Alfonso Rodriquez y Trevisa y Gonsalez, as he styled himself, was apparently content to let Faulkner undertake all the planning and even the final execution of any plan to free the captives. Faulkner asked, 'Tell me, Marie, are the children held in a hut or tent or anything of that nature? Or are they sleeping in the open air?'

'They got a few wickiups and a tent or two there. The girls are all linked together by their wrists, hand-cuffed one to the other in a line.'

'That any grown man could treat children so reduces any compunction I should have felt about taking decisive action. Their blood will be upon their own heads if they begin anything in the line of shooting.'

It was increasingly plain to them all that without Marie to guide them, they would have stood not the remotest chance of finding their way in the canyons of Palo Duro. The path forked, twisted and sometimes appeared to double back on itself. Marie moved swiftly, darting from place to place, even leading them into what they thought, at first, was a cave. It was only a short tunnel in the rock, though, barely ten feet high, which, after twenty feet, opened out again into an open track.

Judging by the moon, it must have lacked only an hour to midnight when

Marie halted them and explained in a whisper that they were only a mile or so from the camp, which lay straight ahead. She gave it as her intention to wait where they were, look after the horses for the men and not become embroiled in any of the bloodshed and violence.

The four men walked on slowly, keeping to the shadows, until, on a rocky outcrop a hundred yards ahead of them, they saw the outline of a man sitting with what looked to be a rifle in his arms. Faulkner touched each man on the arm to signal that they should stop. He then came on at a slow stroll. The man was not the world's best sentry, because the minister had to draw attention to his presence when he was practically on top of him. He halted and called out softly, 'Mahrooway,' which is as much as to say, 'Hallo,' in Taibo.

The man on guard stood up, cocked his piece and pointed it towards Faulkner. 'Kwai toh say amigo?' he called. Are you a friend?

The three men behind Faulkner caught snatches of a conversation and then saw the pastor walking up to the man. For a brief moment, the two of them were silhouetted in the moonlight and then one of the figures made a rapid movement and the other fell down. The three of them sprinted forward, hoping that it was the minister who had triumphed. So it proved when they reached them, because a rough-looking man was lying on top of the rock, unconscious and breathing stertorously.

The pastor had a large rock in his hand and a regretful expression on his face. 'Had to do it,' he announced sorrowfully. 'He smelled a rat and went for to fire, so I lamped him with a rock. I think he will live, but you men had better truss him up tight. A gag wouldn't go amiss, either.' It escaped nobody's notice that now that the action had begun, Faulkner was speaking like a man giving orders. The elderly parson had all but melted away, leaving only a grim-looking man that none of the other three felt inclined to cross.

According to what the girl had told them, the camp itself would be another hundred yards or so ahead of them. If Faulkner was right and the men were getting liquored up in the Comanche village, then they would only have one or at the most two more men to deal with. All the men had their pistols out now, although their fervent hope was that it would not come to shooting. The sound of a gun battle erupting in the canyons would be sure to bring every Comanche, Kiowa and Comanchero for fifty miles running in their direction, an eventuality that all four hoped to avoid.

They moved on cautiously, stopping at intervals to listen. Far off in the distance was the faint sound of singing and occasional shouts. It was difficult to judge distances in the canyon, but to Faulkner it sounded as though the noise was coming from at least a couple of miles away. He indicated that the others should stop.

'I will now go on ahead again by myself. I do not wish to take the chance of one of you young bucks opening fire. It would be like sticking our heads in a hornets' nest.' He reached under his coat and pulled out the Bowie knife. 'I will hope to reason with anybody who I meet and if that does not serve, I shall cut his throat. I hope it won't come to that.'

There was something extraordinarily chilling about hearing an elderly man clad in clerical black talking in this fashion. When he mentioned the possibility of cutting a man's throat, there was not the slightest doubt in the minds of those hearing him that he meant this quite literally and that in order to rescue the children, he would be quite willing and able to kill anybody who stepped in his path.

Faulkner spoke again. 'God willing, we shall be able to conclude this business in an hour. Tell me now, you boys, are you aiming to take this gold from the Comancheros, if you can find it, or is it really your intention just to report to the nearest lawman where it might be found? You best not fool with me now; I'm in a hurry.'

The two men shrugged. 'Bit of both, I guess,' said one. 'We thought of taking some of it and then tracking them as they move it to a town.'

'Just wait here, then, and you can do that once those girls are freed. And you, Gonsalez, you can wait here, too. If I free the children, I shall also have the two women. None of you come on until I say so.'

Faulkner moved silently along the side of the rock face, keeping the little huddle of wickiups in sight. As he got closer, he saw a flurry of movement and heard a high, childish cry of distress. He moved swiftly forward until he was in the Comanchero camp itself. As he moved round the first wickiup, Faulkner both saw what had caused the movement and understood the distressed cry he had heard. Two figures were lying in the dust, struggling. One was a grown man who was snarling and grunting with frustration as he tried to force himself on a slim girl. At first, Faulkner assumed that it was some camp follower of the Comancheros, maybe a girl like Marie from the saloon. Then the two of them rolled over and he could see that the girl was a mere child. With a dreadful shock he suddenly realized what he was witnessing; the attempted violation of one of the children from the Oneida Orphans' Asylum.

Twenty years ago, Jonas Faulkner's temper had been legendary. Even among men who would kill somebody at the drop of a hat over some fancied slight, Faulkner was regarded with some caution. He had been known to explode in a killing rage for almost nothing, firing randomly at anybody in sight. People took good care in the old days not to piss Jonas Faulkner off.

For the first time in over fifteen years, Faulkner's devil was loosed. He sprang at the villain, who was trying to rape the girl who could be thirteen at most, and hauled him off the child. The man's back was to him as he whirled him round, and without pausing for a fraction of a second the preacher grabbed a hold of the man's lank and greasy hair and jerked his head back sharply. Then he brought his Bowie knife round and slashed his throat with as much force as he could muster.

The blood shot out from the severed arteries in the man's neck with enough force to send it spurting three foot into the air. Faulkner did his best not to get in the way of this fountain, thrusting the man from him with disgust. The child was watching the scene in terror, obviously wondering if she was about to become the next victim of this knife-wielding maniac. The pastor sheathed his knife and squatted down next to her.

'It's all right, child, don't be afeared. I've come to take you on to the orphans' asylum in Claremont. Did yon ruffian . . . did he . . . ?'

'No, sir, but it weren't for want of trying!'

'So I saw. Come on, there's a good girl. I know you've had a shock, but we need to be moving quickly now.'

'Is he dead?'

'Well, I don't think he'll be troubling any more girls in that way in a hurry.'

At that moment, the other three men fetched up in the camp, in flat defiance of Faulkner's clear instructions to them. The first on the scene was the nicest looking of the two boys, who almost tripped over the bloody corpse of the Comanchero. He looked down to see what had caused him to stumble and then gave a low moan when the horror of the thing struck him. The man's head was only just hanging onto his shoulders by a thin band of flesh and skin. 'Jesus Christ!' he exclaimed in horror. 'You nearly took his head off!'

'Well, boy, I told you I would cut any man's throat who hindered my objective. Strikes me you are a mite too squeamish for this sort of work.'

The other two men stood dumb-struck as they gazed down at the all but decapitated body. They looked from the body to the preacher and then back again. It was pretty plain that they were all three of them wondering what sort of man they had hitched up with. In the meantime, Faulkner was tenderly help-ing the young girl up and speaking soft and comforting words to her. He put his arm round her shoulders and, ignor-ing the others, began to help her in the direction of where she said her friends were being kept.

The five girls and two women were all handcuffed together and the last two in the line were each handcuffed to the wheel of a wagon. The girl he was supporting had a handcuff dangling from her wrist and it was a fair guess that the man who had been trying to ravish her had freed her from the line. This meant that he must have a key, which would unlock the cuffs. Faulkner turned to the three men. 'One of you run now and search that devil I killed. Bring back the key, which he must have about him.' None of the three made any attempt to obey.

'I ain't going near to that thing!' said one of the young men, and his companions evidently felt the same way.

The preacher clucked an irritable noise in his throat. 'Landsakes, what's wrong with you all? A dead man can't hurt you. What is it, you all afraid of the bogeyman? Stay here, I'll go myself.'

But Pastor Faulkner did not get the opportunity to fetch the key, because he was suddenly aware that the ground was trembling in the way it did when a troop of horses were coming along at a smart pace. By the time he had grasped the implications of this, a dozen men on horseback were thundering into the camp and had surrounded the minister and his travelling companions. Faulkner raised his hands and the others followed suit. All the riders had pistols, shotguns or rifles trained on them; it would have been suicide to set to under those circumstances.

A pleasant-looking and portly middle-aged man with immaculately trimmed mustachios dismounted and stood for a moment surveying the four of them. From a little way off came an exclamation of anger. They had discovered the man that the minister had killed. The fellow who had got off his horse went to investigate, leaving the other horsemen keeping their weapons trained upon the four intruders. When he returned, this man, who seemed to be the leader of the others, said in perfect English, with only the faintest of Spanish accents, 'Tell me, which of you killed him?'

'I did.'

'Remarkable. You have nearly severed his head from his body. What did you use?'

'I will show you, but I must reach under my coat. Tell your men to be easy, I'm not going for a gun.' The pastor brought out his Bowie knife and tossed it down in front of the mustachioed man, who picked it up and examined it carefully.

'It is a fine weapon. Why did you kill him?'

'He had freed this child and was trying to force himself upon her. I would kill him again if I saw such a thing. He was a beast who deserved to die.'

'What you say is true and I would not have left him alone to guard these people, had I been here. You have saved me five hundred dollars and the trouble of killing the man myself. The value of these girls lies chiefly in their virginity. A used girl drops in price dramatically. Thank you.'

The other riders were dismounting now and were staring in no friendly fashion at the men who had crept into their camp and killed one of their number. The leader gestured to the four prisoners and said, 'Stand over there please, in a line. I wish to know what is going on here. You are not soldiers, that is certain. You, old man, where did you

116

learn to use a Bowie knife in that way? I know some knife-fighters, indeed I have killed many myself with a blade, but I have never yet seen anybody served so. What is your profession?'

'I am a Presbyterian minister. I look after the church in Claremont, some miles north of here.'

'Claremont. Ah yes, that is where those girls were headed, is it not? And you are really a priest? Yes, I see by your clothes that it could be so. And yet what a priest! I have only dealt in the past with Catholic priests and they are not like you at all. Few of them would take off a man's head as you did. Are all Presbyterians that fierce?'

'Happen it depends which theological college they attended.'

The Comanchero leader roared with laughter, slapping his leg with delight. He might have been a man attending a musical theatre for all the honest enjoyment the discussion of the near beheading of one of his band seemed to have given him. 'I like you, Father. I might have to kill you shortly, but that will not lessen my liking, I do assure you.'

'It ain't necessary to call me 'Father'. We don't go a bunch on such goings on in our church.'

'Forgive me. As I say, I have met few priests other than those who are Catholic. But now to business. Gentlemen, would you please step forward one at a time and lay down your weapons?' The four men each did so.

'And now, perhaps you could explain to me why you have invaded our privacy? I am inclined to view such trespass with extreme disfavour, especially as we are currently enjoying a period of relaxation with our friends, the Comanche. You are nothing to do with General Sheridan and yet here you are, blundering into our hideout. What is the meaning of it?'

None of the prisoners spoke. The Comanchero pulled a pistol from the holster at his hip and shot dead one of the two younger men. It was done with shocking swiftness and before the echo of the shot had died down, the boy was lying motionless on the ground.

'Ah, you men think that because I speak pleasantly, you can ignore my questions. Not so.' He turned to one of the riders. 'Tico, ride over to the village and tell them not to be alarmed by the shot. Tell them that I am questioning some prisoners and that they should not be worried if they hear three more shots. Any more than that and it will mean an attack.' The man thus addressed rode off in haste. The leader spoke once more. 'Again, what is the meaning of this?'

The Portuguese man who had given his name as Gonsalez stepped forward a few paces. 'Señor, I am here by arrangement. We have corresponded and you agreed to ransom my sister for two hundred and fifty dollars in gold. I have it with me.'

Pastor Faulkner could not restrain himself and burst out at this point. 'You're a rare scoundrel. You mean that

119

you had agreed a ransom and then hoped to tag along with us and save yourself the cost? You crawling snake.'

The Comanchero smiled in delight. 'Ah now, what is this? Has somebody tried to cheat me? Tell me what this means?' Gonsalez began to stutter an excuse, but the leader of the Comancheros silenced him with an imperious gesture. 'No, my friend, not you. Let the priest explain what has taken place. I trust him more than I do you. I think you are a man who will lie as readily as you would speak the truth. Well, sir?' He turned to Faulkner, who gave a brief account of the Portuguese man's actions. There were a few seconds' silence.

'But this is most pleasing. We had a deal and you reneged on it. No, no,' said the Comanchero as Gonsalez tried to protest, 'I can see the truth written on your face. Along with terrible fear. You think that I might kill you for your treachery. Not so, I am no more than a humble businessman. All the same, I think that this provides some grounds for renegotiating the terms of our agreement. Fetch the sister.'

After some discussion, the key was fetched and a young woman of about thirty was brought forward. In the meantime, two men caught hold of Gonsalez and expertly went through his pockets. There, they discovered not only a soft leather pouch containing the ransom money in gold coins, but also another couple of hundred dollars in banknotes. An elaborate gold pocket watch was also removed, along with a cigar cutter, several rings that he was wearing and even his cufflinks. These were all brought forward and handed to their leader.

'There are, Alfonso Rodriquez y Trevisa y Gonsalez, certain penalties in business for those who fail to act in a straightforward and honourable way. In this case, that penalty is merely a financial one, in that we shall take all your belongings in addition to the ransom that we agreed. I tell you now, though, if ever you cross my path again, I shall not hesitate to shoot you down like the treacherous, mangy dog that you are. Be off with you, before I change my mind!'

The Portuguese man and his sister set off back to where Marie had been left in charge of the horses. The children and the remaining teacher had also had their handcuffs removed and were now milling about in a reasonably cheerful way. A fire had been kindled a few yards away and it was obvious that a meal was being prepared. Faulkner and the young man were uncertain what would happen to them now, but the man who was seemingly in charge of the whole camp set their minds at rest, at least for a spell, by saying agreeably, 'It may well come to pass that I shall be forced to kill you both, just in the way of business, as you might say. There is, however, no reason why you should die hungry. Will you join us for food? You others, you little ones and you, teacher, come also near to the fire and we shall all eat.'

Once the fire was blazing merrily, the whole crowd of them sat around it. It surprised Faulkner that the children and their teacher did not seem to be in any particular fear of the men, who did not come across as an especially brutal or depraved bunch. The leader, whose name was Felix, invited the preacher to sit beside him. They ate hunks of bread and slices of meat, which were roasted in the fire. After a while, Felix said, 'Tell me, priest, I can guess why you have come here, but what would you do if I just turned you loose now and sent you back to Claremont? No, don't answer me. I can see in your eyes what would happen. You would go off and then come back in the middle of the night and cut off my head! Is it not so?'

Pastor Faulkner nodded his head slowly. 'I reckon you have figured the case out about right. Tell me, are you not disgusted to be trafficking women and children in this way? Is it a worthy occupation for a man such as you?' To

Faulkner's amazement, the bandit looked crestfallen and ashamed when he heard these words, and ducked his head. Faulkner wondered if he was blushing.

The man looked up and said in a low voice, 'Of course you are right, but what would you do? If I do not provide my men with money and liquor, they will become discontented. The next thing to happen is that it will be said that I have become soft and before you know it there will be a knife in the dark and Raul or Enrique will be leading the group instead of me. What should I do with you?'

The preacher did not get a chance to answer, because just then there were cries of greeting as Marie came into sight, leading four horses. She was obviously well known to the men present and they competed with each other to invite her to sit next to them. She ignored the young man she had slept with earlier that very day, nodded saucily to Faulkner and then came over and kissed Felix demurely on the cheek.

Pastor Faulkner shook his head sadly, but there was an air about him of a man quietly satisfied that he has been shrewder than those around him. 'I knew that you would play us false. I did not trust you from the first, when you so near got me shot. I feel sorry for this young man, for it strikes me that he has fallen for you, fool that he is. Were you working for these brigands the whole time?'

The girl tilted her head defiantly. 'I must make my own way in the world, Preacher. You need not bother to judge me; you have sins enough on your head.'

'That at least is true. Still and all, I could wish that a young person like you made more of herself than a bandit's mistress.'

The girl turned on him savagely. 'Bandit's mistress, is it? What do you think I could do in the sort of nice town where you come from? I could not even get a job as a lady's maid. I am a bastard orphan; nobody knows who my father was. I would be lucky to earn enough to eat. Here I am happy, here I am somebody. I am Marie. Sometimes I work in the saloon, other times I help out my friends here. You tend to your own affairs, Preacher.'

Felix laughed. 'You know, Reverend, she has a point. You tell me that I am a villain for trading in young girls, but Marie was once such a one. She was an orphan, then a whore in a Mexican brothel and now . . . what are you now, my dear?' Marie stalked off, offended, and Felix chuckled again before turning back to Faulkner. 'What is that young companion of yours about? Hoping to steal from us or turn us into the law for money?'

'Something of the sort. Turn him free. He is a good boy and your friend Marie deceived him.'

'Marie! She deceives everybody, that one. I don't know what I shall do with the pair of you. I should have shot you all earlier, but I can hardly murder you now after sitting down to eat with you.'

Faulkner said nothing and just watched the man curiously. He had known a good many villains in his day, but this one seemed to be of a different stamp from most.

'How about this,' said Felix, after thinking the matter over. 'I allow you and your friend to live for the night and then work out what is to be done in the morning. I shall have to handcuff you and bind your feet, but that is, I think you will agree, a more pleasant prospect than being shot dead this minute? Most of us are bound for the Comanche village and so I shall bind you and then leave you and the other captives here under the guard of two men. Does this sound fair?'

There was little more to be said, because the alternative was, as Felix had suggested, instant death.

7

Now, Pastor Faulkner had found spending the night sleeping rough enough of a trial a couple of days ago. Repeating the experiment with his feet tied together and his hands handcuffed behind his back did not make a night on the ground any more comfortable — quite the reverse. He tossed and turned, from time to time doing all those things that any normal man would attempt under the circumstances: namely, trying to untie his feet and free himself from the cuffs. The Comancheros, though, knew their business too well to make a botch of a simple matter such as trussing up a captive so that he couldn't get away in the night.

Judging by the moon, it was three or four in the morning when Faulkner was roused by a groan of pain, followed by a strange gurgling sound. 'Come on, wake up, old man!' a heavily accented voice urged him. 'We have to get moving.' The ropes round his ankles were cut through and his hands were freed. The fire had died down, but in the glow from the embers he could see a huge, Spanish-looking fellow, who was now moving on to the other prisoners. Faulkner got to his feet, rubbing his wrists and becoming aware of the aching in his bones. He could not be sleeping out of doors too many more times before he went down with ague or similar.

'What's the game?' asked the preacher of the Comanchero.

'No game. I am freeing you and you must go. I cannot give you more than a few hours' headstart.' The man turned to the children and the teacher he had freed. 'Come on, get up, move, hurry!'

Faulkner saw at once what the scheme was. He said to the man, 'I am guessing that your name is either Raul or Enrique?'

'How do you know this? I am Raul. Who told you?'

'Your captain mentioned your name

last night. He is expecting you to betray him in some way.'

'Aye, aye, he might well. There will not be a better chance than this. Already, there are some mutterings that we should have killed you at once. Also, Felix is getting tender-hearted about the girls. Nobody will take it well if he gives up three and a half thousand dollars so. I do not think that he will still be leading our band after this night's work. Are you ready?'

Raul led them a little way in the right direction. The children were sleepy and two of the younger ones were crying. The Comanchero took them as far as where their three horses were standing and then left without bidding them farewell or goodnight or any of the usual civilities. The teacher, a tough-looking woman of thirty or so, was shepherding her charges along gently but firmly. It was plain to Faulkner that she was afraid that there would be some outbreak of hysteria among the girls unless they could get away fast. The young man was the only one of them who looked in the least happy. He gave the impression of a man enjoying himself. He had probably, reflected the preacher, not expected to live more than another few hours.

'Get the smaller children up on these horses,' Faulkner said to the teacher, 'we have to be making tracks fast. Come on, ma'am, let's move it.'

Between the three adults, they managed to get three of the children mounted on the horses and then set off at a brisk walk. While lifting one of the littlest ones onto Jenny, the minister had been pleased to note that his keg of black powder had not been looted. It and the fuse were still in one of the saddle-bags. At a guess, he would suppose that they had not known what was in the little wooden barrel.

At the back of Pastor Faulkner's mind, a plan was taking shape. He did not trust any of the band who had been holding the children and it struck him that the man Raul meant them no better than the rest. The best assumption to work on would be that a posse of armed bandits would come galloping after them in an hour or two at the most. They would be lucky to have reached the end of the canyon by that time. Faulkner tried to think back to the days when he himself was up to tricks of this sort. What would he have done in Raul's place? The answer did not take too long to come to him. He would pretend to discover the prisoners having escaped and murdered the guards. Then he would ride after them with some other men in order to recapture them. In the confusion, he would make sure that all the adults were killed and trust that the children would be too frightened to be able to explain clearly the circumstances of their escape — even assuming that they understood what had happened at all.

Lord, thought the preacher to himself, this is a hard row to hoe. I must ensure at all costs that those children are taken to safety, but we are still upwards of twenty or thirty miles from a town. I will never be able to get them out of danger. I am guessing now that I must do my best to give the little ones a chance to get away, even if that means that I am killed in the process. Still and all, Lord, this is not a time for saying, 'Let this cup pass from me,' and so on. I must do what is needful and if that means an end to me, then so be it. It cannot be helped.

Pastor Faulkner called to the teacher, 'Ma'am, could I have a private word with you?'

She brought the horse she was leading closer to Faulkner. 'Well, sir, what's on your mind?'

The preacher lowered his voice almost to a whisper. He did not want to start a panic among the children. 'We are not all going to be able to get clear before the storm breaks. Do you apprehend my meaning?'

'Perfectly. I had thought the same thing myself. Those rascals will be upon us before we are clear of Palo Duro.

What is your intention? You are a resourceful, if bloody, man. Had I known that you were prone to slicing the heads off those who crossed you, I am far from convinced that I should have considered the Claremont Orphans' Asylum to be a suitable place for my charges.'

Faulkner smiled in the darkness. This was a woman who seemingly had no fear at all. 'Here is what I propose. We must find a narrow spot where I can delay any pursuers. You and the children will then move on as fast as you may and trust in God to bring you to safety.'

'What of that young man? Will he stay with us or defend the way alongside you?'

'I know not. He is only a chance companion; I do not know what his purposes are.'

'Do you have anywhere in mind for this ambush you plan?' asked the teacher, just as casually as if she were planning a good spot for a nature study outing.

'The road out of the canyon passes through a cave or tunnel. This will be by way of a bottleneck and if I can hold them there, they will not be able to get after you and the children.'

'It is a hare-brained enough scheme, but I see there is no other choice. Do you have a firearm?'

'That is, you might say, the weak point in the plan. I do not have a weapon, except for a small pistol of the derringer type. It only has two shots and is not accurate at much more than six feet. There is an ace in the hole, though. I have a five-pound barrel of gunpowder and a length of fuse. I might be able to rig something up.'

As they plodded along, Faulkner was aware that the woman was staring fixedly at him, although he could not see her clearly in the darkness. After a space, he said, 'Well, ma'am, are you game? Or will you be playing the fainting game or having the vapours or some such?'

'Ha, you impudent man. I never fainted in the whole course of my life and I ain't about to start at this stage.

Are you planning to blow yourself up as well?'

'I hope not, but it might come to that.'

'I hope you don't. It would be a great loss to the Presbyterian Church. Do you have a tinderbox or ought to light this precious fuse of yours?'

'You anticipate me, ma'am. I was just about to ask you.'

'That young scallywag has some lucifers. I'll fetch them for you.'

According to Pastor Faulkner's calculations the cave through which they had passed would take fifteen minutes more to reach. He had not set much mind to it when they had passed through before, but he recollected that the roof of the thing was pretty low and that there were boulders and piles of loose rocks within it and around the entrances at either end. Five pounds of black powder would not be enough to bring down the roof and seal the cave, of that he was sure. If he was going to cause an explosion, then it would have to be one aimed directly at the men he felt sure would be galloping after them in a short time. In other words, he would have to commit a massacre if there was to be any chance of saving the children.

This gloomy train of thought was interrupted by the teacher, who said, 'Would your job be easier if I was to stay and help? That young fellow might be able to take my girls onwards.'

'It's kind of you, ma'am, but I would not trust that boy to look after my cat for the day. He is apt to bolt and abandon them in the wilderness. I am mightily obliged to you for the offer, but I would a sight rather know that you had charge of the little ones and were tending to their needs.'

They were now almost at the entrance to the short tunnel, which would bring them to the track leading out of Palo Duro.

'Let's rest here a minute,' said the preacher, 'and collect our thoughts. Gather round, you children, and listen to what I am about to tell you. Your teacher, this good woman, is going to take you on to the town of Claremont, where you were headed before this adventure befell you. You might get hungry or thirsty on the road, but that is no matter. It is enough that you are out of the reach of those villainous men. Now, collect yourselves for a moment, while I have a short private conference with my friend here.' He led the young fellow out of earshot and then addressed him thus.

'I do not know who you are or what your plans might be, but if you are any sort of man at all, you will accompany that woman and those children and take care of them. If you fail to do so, your conscience will afflict you and if that is not sufficient inducement, then I tell you straight, you will answer to me for it. You have seen how I serve those who get in my way; I do not think you would wish to get crosswise to me. If you run from this duty, I will hunt you down and kill you.'

'Hey, Preacher, you've no call to talk so! I wouldn't shirk my duty. Be sure, I will stay with these children.'

Pastor Faulkner went over to the teacher and spoke a few final words to her. 'You must leave right now. I do not think that there is any time to lose.'

The woman reached out and gripped Faulkner's arm with such fierce strength that he winced. 'I hope that we shall meet again.'

'It may be so, ma'am, it may be so. Now be off. The young man is going with you, but it is not clear to me how much you can rely upon him.'

The man, woman and six children set off through the short tunnel, taking with them two of the horses and leaving Jonas Faulkner to set to work. He began to hump rocks from all over and built a cairn right in the middle of the cave's entrance. Before he started on this endeavour, he walked Jenny through the tunnel and fixed her bridle securely to an old, iron-hard bristlecone pine, which was growing just on the other side of the cave. Then he took the keg of powder and the length of fuse out of the saddlebag, checked that the little muff pistol was ready and loaded and went back to begin his labours.

It had been some few years since Faulkner had engaged in heavy manual work of this type. He tried to roll some of the larger rocks, rather than lifting them, but the effort was still enough to reduce him to a trembling, sweat-soaked old man within ten minutes. 'Jonas,' he muttered to himself, 'you are out of condition and that's a fact. You have, as the saying goes, let yourself go over the years.'

After he had been working for a while, Faulkner managed to build a ring of large rocks, each three or four times the size of a man's head. This ring had a space maybe two feet wide in the middle. Here he placed the keg of powder and surrounded it with more rocks and pebbles.

Before he laid his mine, Faulkner tested the fuse and tried to figure out how long he should make it. He cut a length of fuse a foot long by sawing it on a jagged rock and then set fire to the end. It gave him ten seconds. The problem was that he needed to give himself time enough to get clear, but not so long that anybody could see what the game was and get clear themselves. Nor would it work if the Comancheros stood off from the cave mouth to see what was happening. He needed them to be in hot pursuit of him, but perhaps twenty-five yards behind. It would take some thinking.

In the end, he decided that ten seconds would do the trick and he fixed the fuse into the bung at the top of the keg, leaving plenty of space round it so that it would burn well. The end product was a cairn of stones about two feet high. In front of this, he rolled a couple of boulders, large enough for him to crouch behind. He had a strong suspicion that the man called Felix would not be one to miss the deadly significance of the artfully constructed pile of rocks. The boulders, however, both screened the mine from view and also gave him a vantage point from which to fire.

He had barely completed his preparations before becoming aware of a faint rumbling in the distance, which portended the arrival of the bandits. Pastor Faulkner crouched behind the boulders and pulled out the little derringer and the box of lucifers. He was ready for action.

8

Gauging it from the sound, the preacher reckoned that there must be about eight or ten men in the party and when they came into view around the rocks, he was pleased to see that he had been pretty well spot on. Eight riders pulled up some five and twenty yards from the cave mouth. They had seen the two large boulders and were obviously wondering what might be going on. It was time, thought Faulkner, to put them on the back foot. He doubted that they had seen him yet in the glimmering half-light of dawn and so he still had an advantage; an advantage which he meant to exploit to the full.

The little pistol, which was clasped in his hand, was not accurate above six feet or so. It was designed only to be used at close quarters, when somebody posing a threat was right on top of you.

However, the cartridge it fired, the .41, was powerful enough to carry a good long way and still have the energy to kill a man a hundred yards off. Mind, if you shot anybody at that distance it would be sheerest chance and no credit to your marksmanship.

Pastor Faulkner could hear the men talking, trying to figure out if there might be a threat ahead of them. At last, they made up their minds and there was a jingling of bridles as they prepared to move towards him. It was at that point that he loosed off a shot in the general direction of the riders. He was highly gratified when the bullet took a man, who then fell from his horse. It still left the preacher facing seven desperate men, but it had improved the odds by a fraction. Only thing was, the little muff pistol only chambered two rounds. One was now gone, which left him with a single shot.

The result of his lucky shot was only what could be expected: the bunch of riders split off in all directions, racing for cover. Well, all directions except for one, which was towards the cave. None of the men durst show themselves, but the familiar voice of their leader, Felix, hailed him from cover. 'Father, I make not the least doubt that it was you who just shot at us. What will you have? Do you want to take us all on single-handed?'

'I ain't alone and I am ready for every man jack of you as wants to try his luck. You want to come first?'

'I am in no hurry. I shall take the children on the road, even if we parlay here for an hour. You know this; why not give us the road? I do not wish to kill you.'

'I killed those men who you set a-guarding of us last night. You think I would not kill the whole crew of you? Walk on and give it a go.'

Felix roared with laughter; it sounded as though he was genuinely amused by the situation. 'You didn't kill those guards, Father. I know who was answerable for that. It was my old friend Raul.'

'Raul?' called back Faulkner. 'That

name does not bring anybody to mind.'

There was some more conversation amongst the men and then, quite unexpectedly, somebody swung a large, rock-like object in Faulkner's direction. The thing skidded and rolled, coming to rest half a dozen yards from him. It was nearly light now and Faulkner could see clearly what the object was. It was a human head and by chance the face, with its sightless eyes, was turned towards him. It was the man who had freed him and the other prisoners a few hours earlier.

'What do you say, Father? You did not mind me trying out that Bowie knife of yours, I trust? I have never killed a man so. The older we grow, the readier should we be to try new experiences, wouldn't you say so?'

'Keep down your present road, Felix, and you are apt to experience something right novel, which will amount to a bullet from me through your head. Back up, I say. Return to your camp and you will not be harmed.'

'I do not think that you have much ammunition,' observed Felix shrewdly. 'My men are showing themselves and you do not seem to be shooting at them. How many bullets do you have left, Father?'

This was all getting a sight too near to the knuckle for Faulkner's liking. He cried, 'I got enough bullets, don't you fret about that!' and fired his remaining shot towards the rocks where the men were sheltering. The result was a perfect fusillade of fire directed at the boulders behind which he was crouched. He bent even lower and put his arms over his head to shield against any ricochets. It was almost time for his last throw.

Although the light was brightening by the minute, it was still a fair guess that the men trying to force a passage through the cave could not actually see him, where he was crouched down behind the two large boulders. They had concealed themselves again and for all they knew to the contrary, he might have bolted into the cave itself and be hiding there now. He squashed himself up as small as he could, managing to get himself so that he could still peek out from the narrow space between the two boulders.

'Father, we must be moving now,' called Felix, 'I have been patient with you and though I do not want the death of a priest on my conscience, I shall have to insist that you surrender.'

Faulkner stayed perfectly still and did not answer. The Comancheros were not overmuch keen on showing themselves, since as far as they knew a desperate man lay behind cover and ready to shoot them down if they approached. There was some cursing as Felix drove them on and after a few seconds the party had assembled and were walking forward at a slow and cautious pace. 'Well, Jonas,' said Faulkner quietly, 'it's now or never, boy.' He lit the fuse.

The seven horsemen came on at an agonizingly slow pace and the minister did not dare to show himself or do anything which would cause them to slow down or halt. He guessed that the fuse was now burned about halfway through and it was the perfect time for him to cut and run. He leaped up and sprinted back to the cave, jinking and twisting as he ran. A couple of the men fired at him, but they had been so taken aback to see him jump out from concealment that they had not had the chance to aim properly.

There was no sense in turning back to see what the men were doing now. All the preacher could do was run as though the Devil himself were after him. He had judged the length of the fuse a little finer than was comfortable, because he was not out of the other side of the short, rocky tunnel before the explosion caught him and sent him whirling to the ground. He was that close to it that he didn't really hear the blast, just pressure in his ears and then the sensation of being hurled forward.

He lay on the ground, momentarily stunned as the cave filled with smoke and dust. His ears were ringing, but he could hear nothing. There was no sound of horses' hoofs or men shouting. As he recovered himself and stood up, choking in the smoke, he gradually became aware of faint noises of distress. Horses were whinnying, men groaning and a few grunted curses. It was not a good idea to wait round to chew the fat with the survivors and Faulkner forced himself to stagger out into the fresh air.

Jenny was terrified, her eyes wide open and foam flecking her mouth. She had been rearing and jittering and if the old pine had not been rooted so deeply in the rock, she would have torn it loose for sure. He soothed the frantic creature and then untied her from the tree. Nobody was following him, that much seemed certain, and so he mounted the mare and headed west towards the road between Oneida and Claremont. For the first time since he had engaged to undertake this mission, Pastor Faulkner was beginning to feel that he might actually have a chance of succeeding.

It was likely that the children could

not be more than twenty minutes' ride ahead of him and the minister was feeling right braced with the world. Not in a prideful and worldly way, you understand, just the sober satisfaction of having been set a task by the Lord and having fulfilled it to the best of his ability. He caught up with the party in ten minutes. They had stopped to rest when they saw him approaching and the teacher walked towards him, partly with the intention of greeting him, but also, he suspected, for a private conference upon their next step.

'Well, ma'am,' he said, 'I would have thought that you might be more advanced upon the way than this. Have you stopped for a rest or something of that sort? This is not a Sunday School treat, you know.'

'What a mercy you weren't killed in that explosion we heard. I take it that was your doing and not the bandits'?'

'It was.'

'What of the men? Are they still on our track?'

Pastor Faulkner looked back. 'I see no signs of pursuit. Could be it has discouraged them. They might have thought better of chasing you.'

'Did you kill them all?'

'Truth to tell, ma'am, I do not know. 'Whosoever rolleth a stone, it shall return upon him'. Proverbs, twenty-five, verse twenty-six. Those boys surely rolled a stone when they stole those children off the public highway. I would not waste your grief on them.'

'What is to be done now? I tell you, those girls will not be able to walk all day without food or water. They are scared and thirsty and it will be a miracle if the younger ones don't faint or something.'

'I had thought on this. It is not an easy matter.'

'Well, that takes us no further along the road. What do you advise?'

'Why, ma'am, to keep moving for now. That explosion will have attracted attention from all and sundry within a ten-mile radius. It will be the full moon tonight, a Comanche Moon. Those Indians will be out raiding before dusk and if they find us on the road, we are lost.'

Faulkner dismounted and helped the two youngest girls onto Jenny. Then, once they were on the move again, he went up to the young man and took him aside. 'Well, you have played the man so far, for which I am thankful. We are not yet out of the woods, though, and I wish to consult with you. Apart from Santa Pueblo, where is the nearest settlement?'

'Preacher, I am not from around here, but as far as I can tell, there is a small town, more like a hamlet, about twelve miles from here. It is only a few houses and a well, though. It would not be defensible if a band of determined men attacked.'

'Do you know any source of water or food near here? How much is in the canteens on the horses?'

'Hardly any. I am telling you that once the sun is fairly up, those children will drop like flies from hunger, thirst and tiredness. They have all been up since three in the morning, same as us, you know.'

'I had not forgot it. Do you have any ideas on how to proceed? I am out of condition and it is a long while since I tried anything of this sort.'

'I would say that your 'out of practice' is better than I could manage myself. I have no ideas on what is to become of our party. I think that a bunch of Indians will soon descend upon us. We shall be killed and then they will seize the girls and sell them back to the Comancheros.'

'Yes, that is also what I fear myself. It is a bad business.' The party walked on for two more hours. The end of the Palo Duro Canyon system is not an abrupt change from cliffs and chasms to open land. Instead, it tapers off over the course of some miles. Before they were fairly out of Palo Duro, the preacher spotted a few birds circling down towards a craggy formation half a mile from the track they were on. He told the two adults that he would be back directly and, turfing the two children off Jenny, he mounted and rode off to investigate. A gap in the cliff, no more than fifteen feet wide, led to a natural amphitheatre, at the centre of which was a pond of fresh, clear water. He rode back swiftly to the others.

'There's water over yonder, enough and to spare for us all, including the horses. We can rest up there for a space and let the children regain their strength.'

They all drank their fill of the water, which had somehow accumulated in what looked to be a natural cistern. After the humans had had what they wanted and the canteens had been filled, Faulkner directed that the horses be led round to the other side and allowed to drink. 'Mind they don't foul the water,' he told the young man. He went over to the teacher.

'We have not been what you might call properly introduced, ma'am. The circumstances have been a little strange. I am Jonas Faulkner and I am one of the trustees of the Claremont Orphans' Asylum.' He reached out his hand.

The teacher grasped his hand with surprising strength. 'Martha Weiss. I am one of the teachers, I should say former teachers, at the orphanage in Oneida. I am very pleased to meet you, Reverend Faulkner. Your reputation in Oneida is that of a godly man who is tireless in working for the good of children. Less has been said of your skill with explosives.'

'Merely a hobby, Miss Weiss, I do assure you.' Speaking in general, Faulkner did not engage in chaff of this sort, particularly not with women. There was, though, something about Martha Weiss which encouraged him to be a little playful. He glanced at her surreptitiously. He had, at first, taken her for being about thirty, but in the morning light, she looked nearer to twenty-five.

The children had recovered their spirits to the extent that the three youngest were running round the pool, playing some kind of game. The teacher said, 'It is a marvellous thing to see how quickly children of that age will throw off bad memories. By the time they are eighteen or twenty, they will think no more of this affair than that it was a pleasant holiday. They have no apprehension whatever of the dangers that they have been in.'

'That they are still in, Miss Weiss,' observed Pastor Faulkner. 'We are not out of the trap yet. I cannot decide in my own mind whether we should stay here or move on.'

'Stay for what? We will all grow hungrier by the hour and no closer to safety. You have not hitherto struck me as a vacillating man, one who hesitates to take action.'

Faulkner looked at Martha Weiss and considered for a moment before replying. 'Blunt words, ma'am, blunt words. I will say this. If it were a question of my own safety, I would take a chance now and make a bolt for it, hoping to good fortune. But there are the children to think of. Those rascals had it in mind to sell them to some Mexican brothel, to be used as whores. This would be the worst thing imaginable. I cannot be answerable for putting them in that sort of hazard. Perhaps it would be kinder to stay here and see them die of heatstroke or some such.'

These sentiments stirred the teacher to fury. 'Rouse up, man. Don't let me hear such a notion again. While there is life, there is hope. I will not consent to be party to anything that tends in that direction. I aim to bring those girls safely home to a refuge and if you will not assist me, why then I shall strike out with them by myself.'

'You are in the right, ma'am, in the right. I suggest, though, that we might wait here an hour or so and let us all be thoroughly refreshed.'

'Tell me, does your congregation back in Claremont know what a singular minister they are blessed with?'

Faulkner laughed shortly. 'I would

not have said so, no. They think of me as a dry and self-righteous fellow. Perhaps they are right. I doubt that they would think me capable of striking a man on the cheek, let alone removing his head for him.'

The children had drunk more from the pond and were now sitting in the shade talking in low voices, like they might have been sitting in the school-yard during recess. The young man had perched himself on a rock and was smoking a cigarette. Faulkner said, 'What do you make to that young fellow? You have travelled with him for a few hours now. Would you trust him?'

The teacher considered for a moment. 'He is a deep one, for all his easy ways. I cannot figure what he is about. No, I would not say that I would trust him. Why do you ask?'

'I thought, perhaps, of riding off ahead to scout out the land and see what's what.'

'Reverend Faulkner, I desire you do nothing of the sort. I trust you, but I would not care to be left alone again in the care of that young man.'

'Just as you say. Well, in that case, I suppose we had best think of moving on. I shall go and spy out the land. I will be back directly.' The preacher walked off to the crack in the rocks through which they had gained access to the sheltered pool. Martha Weiss watched him as he left and thought to herself, You're a rare breed, Pastor Faulkner, and no mistake.

9

They set off again, still heading west, before the sun was at its height. The girls were reluctant to move from the pleasant spot around the rock pool, but did as they were bid by their teacher readily enough. Faulkner caught a few words alone with the other man before they started.

'Well, boy,' he said, 'I don't know what plans you might have of your own, if any, but now is surely the time for you to put them into operation. I will not blame you if you want to cut and run now. If we are found out here in the wilderness, it will be a short and bloody affair, with any men butchered and the woman and children taken off as captives. It is my duty to die defending them, but it is not yours.'

'I have done a lot of wrong things in my life, Reverend,' said the young man in a troubled voice. 'I have done some very bad things and recollecting what you told us the other night, concerning your own past history, I am moved to think that it might not be too late for me to take another road. What do you say?'

'What do I say? I say praise the Lord for speaking so to you and softening your heart. It is never too late to change. I should be proof to you of that. If a man like me, given over to all beastliness, can be given a second chance, I feel sure that you can. All that you have done can be forgiven and you can start your life afresh, as innocent as a newborn babe, with all your sins lifted from you.'

'Is this really true, Preacher? Can any man be forgiven like that?'

'If it were not true, son, I should have died of shame and guilt years ago.'

'I will speak more on this later, if we win through. Maybe you could guide me and help me to get right with the world?'

'I will do anything within my power to help you. Anything at all. Nothing rejoices the Lord more than when he finds a lost lamb turning to him in this way. There will be happiness in heaven this day at what you have told me.'

It was accordingly with a much lighter heart that Pastor Faulkner led his little flock back onto the road. Whatever else happened, he had helped to bring at least one person in recent days to a realization of his immortal peril. It looked certain to Faulkner that even if that boy died right now, an unbaptized heathen, his good intentions alone would be enough to save him and secure his admission to the promised land.

They made slow progress, perhaps two miles each hour. With some luck, they might strike the hamlet of which the young man had spoken by nightfall, bar being attacked by redskins or similar misfortune. In fact, when disaster did strike, it was of a wholly unexpected nature. They had gained the rough road leading north to Santa Pueblo. To their left were towering, red sandstone cliffs, while to their right the open country stretched away into the distance.

For some while, the preacher had had the feeling that they were being watched. It was nothing he could put his finger on and yet he was sure that his instincts were not deceiving him. Could it be that along the rocky cliffs and escarpments on their left, someone was moving furtively, as though preparing an ambush? There was no point in saying anything about this to the others and Faulkner was just thinking to himself that he should call a halt and maybe split up the party in the hope that some, at least, might escape, when Martha Weiss said, 'Look, there's a rider heading towards us!'

A small cloud of dust being kicked up showed that a single horseman was making towards them from the direction of Palo Duro. They stood transfixed at the sight, there being little that could be done to prepare for action. Faulkner said, 'Miss Weiss, will you take those girls over to the rocks there? I will meet this person alone.'

'Not alone, Preacher,' said the young man, 'I will stand at your side. If he is an enemy, maybe we can overpower him.'

'I am mightily obliged to you for your offer, son, and I will not say no.'

Neither of them were in the least surprised when the figure on horseback drew nigh and they recognized the rider to be Felix, the leader of the Comancheros. He trotted along without looking to be in any particular hurry and when he reached them, he gave every appearance of being pleasantly surprised to have stumbled unexpectedly across some old friends. He reined in his horse some fifteen feet away from the two men.

'Why, Father, this is a surprise. I did not think that our paths would cross again so soon.'

As far as Pastor Faulkner was

concerned, the enterprise upon which he was engaged was too serious a matter for any fooling around like this. 'What will you have? We are unarmed, as you may see.'

'You know, Father, I think that I am growing to be a little afraid of you?'

'I don't see that at all,' said Faulkner. 'Seems to me as all the cards are in your hand and that it's your turn to lay down. You must do as you see fit; there's little enough that I can do to hinder you.'

'Why now, that is quite true. And yet in the last few hours, you have cost me everything. Did you know that? Twelve hours ago, I had a band of fine men and nobody had ever dared to dispute my leadership. What is now the case? I will tell you. You killed one of my men as soon as you entered our camp. Raul then killed the two men guarding you and your friends in order to make it look as though you yourself had escaped and murdered them. I was not deceived, and killed Raul myself.

Another of my men you shot dead a few hours ago and five more were killed by your infernal device. The two survivors are gravely injured — I doubt they will live without a doctor's care. Since you arrived, ten of my men have died. If my guardian angel had not warned me to hold back at the cave, perhaps I, too, would be dead now.'

'It is an unlucky coincidence, I will grant you,' conceded the preacher. 'I hope that you are not a superstitious man, otherwise you might think that I have brought you a run of ill fortune.'

Felix drew a pistol and cocked it. 'You might think that I hold you at my mercy, and so it looks. But you speak truly, Father. I am indeed a superstitious man and I fear to gun you down unarmed. But we might remedy that. But first, there is your companion. I have no such dread for him as I feel for you.' Saying this, Felix shot the young man in the chest.

The boy staggered back and then collapsed in a heap. Pastor Faulkner rushed over to him, but he could see at once that there were only a few seconds of life remaining. The boy looked up at him, wondering, imploring, and Faulkner said, 'Don't you worry, son. The Lord heard what you said to me earlier and he knows that you were hoping to turn aside from villainy. I promise you now that in a few minutes' time you will be walking the streets of glory.' He took the boy's hand and was rewarded with a squeeze, which signified to him that he had been understood and that his words were appreciated. He said again, 'Don't you worry, now. The Lord is coming to take you home. You are saved.'

The young man gave a deep breath and then released it slowly, his chest sinking. He did not draw breath again and the blood which had been bubbling out of the wound in his breast ceased to flow. The minister stood up and faced the man on horseback. 'You murderous ruffian. That boy never did you harm, why did you shoot him?'

Felix did not reply, but said at length,

'All prudent reasons of policy tell me to shoot you out of hand without giving you any further chance to set the evil eye on my affairs. But I dare not murder you in that way; I am afraid that I will be cursed. I must give you a fair chance. Then, if you are killed in a fair fight, your blood will not be upon my head.'

'You fool,' said the preacher. 'Do you think that you can trick the Lord in this way? God is not mocked.'

'It is not God who I fear, Father. It is the Devil.' The Comanchero dismounted, still keeping a wary eye on Faulkner and his pistol aimed generally in his direction. He reached into a saddlebag and took out the minister's revolver, which Faulkner had never thought to see again.

'Ah,' said Felix, 'I see you recognize your pistol. Is it dear to you? It is not clear to me how a clergyman comes to have a revolver like this, which is very special to him. It is a pity that I shall never be able to hear the story behind

169

this, but I am by way of being in a hurry. I shall kill you and then return to Palo Duro.'

'If you're going to kill me, then you had best get on with it,' said Faulkner. 'You are like a woman, the number of words that you speak. It is not fitting in a man. If you feel you have need to shoot me, then go ahead.'

'What a remarkable man you are, Father,' said Felix admiringly. 'You would have made a marvellous lieutenant. As I say, I fear to kill you unarmed and in cold blood. Here is what I propose to do. I shall make it quite fair and then when you are dead, you will have no occasion to haunt me or speak ill of me in the next world. I shall place my pistol here and yours next to it. We shall both walk fifty paces and then at a signal, we shall each race for our pistol and try to shoot the other. It gives us both the same chance, but I shall even give you an edge. You can call 'Go'. This means that you will start a little before me.'

The preacher looked at the Coman-chero leader in frank amazement.

'Well, I will say this of you. Whatever it is that leads you to adopt this course, it shows that you are a man. Let us proceed.'

Felix removed his own pistol from the holster at his side and laid it carefully down on a flat rock. Next to it, he placed Faulkner's old Navy Colt. Both were single-action; that is to say that the hammers of both would need to be pulled back and cocked before the trigger was pulled. This made the whole proceedings perfectly fair. In addition to this, as Felix had said, Faulkner was to give the signal for the duel to begin, which gave him a very slight edge. The only scope for sharp practice would be if one or the other of them were to take very short, mincing steps from the two weapons, instead of manly strides, thus lessening that man's distance from his gun. Pastor Faulkner did not believe that Felix was a man who would descend to such crafty artifice.

'Well, Father,' said Felix, 'are you ready to start?'

The two men turned back to back and walked slowly away from the pistols. For a fraction of a second, the minister wondered if the unusual circumstances would justify some chicanery on his part, like rushing back without warning and snatching up the pistols before giving the signal to Felix. Perhaps he might have been justified in doing so for the sake of the children, but he scorned to play such a scurvy trick on one who had so far proved himself honourable enough, at least in his dealings with Faulkner. No, he would see the thing through fairly.

After fifty paces, he stopped and turned slowly to face his adversary. Felix smiled at him. 'I wondered if you would run back, grab the guns and shoot me in the back. I am sorry to have had such unworthy thoughts about an honourable man. Tell me when you are ready to start.'

Faulkner was absurdly and against all

reason uneasy in his own mind about the advantage that he had been given. The only right thing to do was to cut that slight edge down as far as he could. 'I am ready,' he said. 'I shall count to three and then cry, 'Go'. Does that suit you?'

'Always such a tender conscience, Father. Are you worried about taking advantage of my good nature? How do you reconcile such a conscience with killing men without blinking?'

The Reverend Faulkner said, 'Never you set mind to my conscience. Worry about your own soul, rather. Are you ready?'

'I am ready.'

'One, two, three, go!'

As soon as the word 'Go' was out of his mouth, but not the smallest fraction of a second earlier, Faulkner sprinted towards the pistols. Felix was faster, as might be expected from a man whose living depended upon his agility and strength. He reached the pistols while Faulkner was still lumbering on with twenty feet to go. The preacher stopped dead as he saw Felix snatch up both the revolvers and, cocking his own piece with his thumb, draw down on Faulkner.

Pastor Faulkner stood still, waiting for the shot that would kill him. Felix was in no hurry, though. He said, 'Was it a fair contest, Father? You don't say that I took advantage of you?'

'No, I don't say that. Will you allow me a moment to pray?'

The minister closed his eyes and said quietly, 'Father, into thy hands I commend my spirit. Amen.' When the shot came, the sound of it echoed back and forth like rolling thunder and bounced from the cliffs half a mile away.

10

The crack of the gunshot caused Faulkner to open his eyes automatically. He was just in time to see the Comanchero's head explode like an over-ripe watermelon. For a moment, the man stood there with his head opened by a large-calibre bullet, his brains splashed down his face. Then he dropped, lifeless, to the ground. Instinctively, Faulkner dived down and plucked up his pistol from where the dead man had dropped it. He lay flat and scanned the surrounding country to see where the shot might have come from.

He glanced anxiously over to the children and, to his amazement, saw half a dozen US cavalry troopers scrambling down from the rocks and talking cheerfully to the teacher and her girls. One of them detached himself and walked over to where Faulkner lay on the ground, still astounded at the turn of events. He stood up and at once recognized the young officer who had brought him news of the capture of the orphanage girls. 'Well, Captain,' he said, 'this is indeed a surprise. When last we spoke, you told me that the army would need to launch a war if they hoped to effect the rescue of those girls. What changed?'

'Nothing changed, Reverend Faulkner, I just did not see the need to vouchsafe to you the details of what we planned to do. When I visited you, I was already under instructions from General Sheridan to gather volunteers and make a stealthy raid on Palo Duro, the aim being to recover those girls without engaging in a full-scale war. If you had stayed at home, we should have been entering the canyons this very day.'

'I am a man who likes to undertake things for himself, Captain. At any rate, here are the children and their teacher.'

'I thought that there were two women with them. Where is the other?'

'She has been ransomed. It is all taken care of.'

'You are a strange one, Pastor Faulkner. I see you are carrying a pistol. How does this tie in with your faith?'

Faulkner felt that it was time to change the topic of conversation. 'Who must I thank for saving my life? I suppose it was one of your men?'

'Yes, would you like to meet him? He is over there.'

The captain led Faulkner over to where the troopers were chatting to the girls and generally making themselves agreeable. 'Cartwright, the preacher here would like to meet the man who saved his life.'

A grizzled-looking man of forty-odd stepped forward. He was carrying a rifle of most unusual design, the barrel being surmounted with a long, narrow brass tube, which ran from the stock to the muzzle. Faulkner had never seen anything like it in his life. 'What kind of weapon is that, if you don't mind me asking?'

'Interested in shooting, are you, sir? Here, have a look. Take it in your hands and feel the weight of it.' Pastor Faulkner took the weapon and hefted it in his hands. It weighed considerably more than the muskets that he remembered using years ago.

'Tell me, now, what make of rifle is this? I do not recollect seeing such a model before.'

'It's a Whitworth,' said the trooper. 'The British made them and sold them to the Confederates. We picked up a few after the war. Beautiful piece of work.'

The preacher felt that he owed the man some appreciation for the shot that had killed Felix and so continued the conversation, though he would sooner have been reassuring the children and exchanging pleasantries with their teacher. 'From what distance was the shot that you made? It looked to me to be some hundreds of yards.'

'Half a mile, Reverend. I can sight up to twelve hundred yards with this baby.'

'She's a muzzle-loader, too, I observe.

178

I suppose that meant that you only had one go at it?'

'Fires a .45-calibre bullet. One shot is all you need if you put it in the right place.'

'You were that confident at such a distance? Eight hundred yards is quite a range. Is it not at the extremity of the weapon's killing range?' In spite of himself, Faulkner was beginning to take his old interest in anything to do with firearms.

'Huh,' said the soldier, 'I can hit a target at twice that distance. The best shot I ever heard tell on was at the Battle of Spotsylvania Courthouse. You ever hear tell of it?'

'I don't recall. What happened?'

'I was there; it was in May 1864. The Confederate lines were the best part of a mile and a half from us, say, two thousand yards at least. They had some men there shooting with Whitworths, just like this one. The bullets were whistling round us, even at that range, and we were sheltering and lying down in the dust, so's not to present a good target. The general, General Sedgwick, that was, he comes up and lights into us for lying down and cowering behind walls. 'I'm ashamed of you boys,' he said to us, 'dodging around like this. Why, they couldn't hit an elephant at this range!' Next thing you know, he has fallen dead, shot straight through his left eye. There are those who say it was a lucky, chance shot, but I don't believe it.'

'Do you not? Why's that?'

'It was a headshot, right in the eye, which is where they train us sharpshooters to aim for.'

'Is that a fact? Surely, though, it could have been a freak?'

'Nothing of the sort,' said the soldier. 'Back about ten years ago, the Queen of England herself scored a bullseye at a quarter-mile range with a Whitworth.'

'Queen Victoria? How's that?'

'It was at their big, annual sharpshooting contest. They call it Bisley. The rifle had been secured in a clamp and all she had to do was pull a string fixed to the trigger, but it goes to show how accurate the thing was. Four hundred and forty yards and it was bang in the bullseye.'

'Well,' said Reverend Faulkner, 'I am very much obliged to you for your actions. If you had not been such a fine shot, the Presbyterian Church in Claremont might have been looking for a new minister.' He handed back the rifle, shook hands with the man and went over to where Martha Weiss was standing and watching her charges chattering to the soldiers. 'Well, ma'am, I think that we might be entering the home straight now, if you'll forgive me for using a sporting expression.'

She turned and looked at him shrewdly. 'Why do you say so?'

'Why, because we have the army here now to protect us and I am sure that they will escort us on our way.'

'Yes, all eight of them. What will happen if a band of thirty or forty Comanches come riding down on us?

You think that those eight men will vanquish them all?'

'You know, Miss Weiss, for a woman you have an uncommon knack for putting your finger right on the crux of a problem. You are, of course, right. Did the captain say where his base was?'

'He did. Forty miles from here. This small party was given permission to enter the canyons by stealth and try to rescue us. There are no other soldiers within forty miles.'

'What a mercy that I have recovered my pistol. I had best take that Comanchero's weapon also.'

'Pistols, pistols! For a man of God, you seem to me to rely a sight too much on firearms and not nearly enough upon prayer.'

'They go hand in hand, ma'am. The Lord helps those who help themselves.'

The cavalry officer came over to Faulkner and the teacher. He said, 'If you have no objection, I say we should be leaving right about now. We have been lucky, but it would greatly ease my mind to be on the road. I have permission to escort you all as far as Claremont.'

'How is this to be done?' asked the preacher.

'We will travel back to Santa Pueblo and lay hands upon a cart. I make no doubt that there will be such a thing there and I have the power to requisition it on behalf of the military, that is to say if the owner will not part with it and sell it to us. Then we can take these children to your orphanage and get back to the serious business.'

Three of the troopers were left to guard the girls and the others went off with the captain to collect the horses. The preacher went over to where Felix lay dead and took the Comanchero's gun from his lifeless hand. Then on an impulse, he went through the man's pockets. There was nothing there of any use and so he tucked the second pistol in his belt along with his own Colt and went back to the teacher. She eyed him with disapproval.

'Well, you look a fine one and no mistake with those two pistols. Why, you look more like a bandit than a clergyman. Whatever do you mean by it?'

'I am not easy in my mind, ma'am. I will be grateful enough for the help of that young officer and his soldiers, but I will also make my own arrangements. It strikes me that you have little enough to complain about my actions so far.'

'That at least is true. Were it not for you, I would probably still be held captive over in Palo Duro. You are not to suppose that I am ungrateful. That is far from being the case.'

'The fact is, Miss Weiss, you and I must still set a watch upon those girls and not hand the task over to others, no matter how tempting it might be to do so. Our duty lies with them and we have no business passing it on. I am sure you fully apprehend my meaning.'

'Of course,' said the teacher, 'I see the case in the same light.'

When the captain came back, it was time to discuss the journey they were to make to Santa Pueblo. Before this, the girls shared some food with the cavalrymen. 'We are travelling light,' the officer told them, 'but what food we are carrying, you are welcome to share.' It was a pleasant enough meal, with the soldiers joshing the girls and trying to make them laugh.

The preacher went to hunt out the young captain. When he found him, he addressed him in this wise. 'Captain, it took us the best part of a day to get here from Santa Pueblo. That was riding at a fair rate, with hardly any stopping. I doubt that we can do this with these children. How do you propose to travel?'

'The girls can ride, of course,' said the officer promptly. 'Which means that the speed will be dictated by how fast we can march. I think that we can make it very late at night today. I don't want to camp out in this territory; it would be madness. It is a Comanche Moon tonight. I dare say that you know what this means.'

Faulkner nodded. 'It means that at dusk, bands of Kiowa and Comanche will issue forth from the canyons in search of plunder. We have perhaps twelve hours of daylight before then and must be as far from here as can be.'

'It is nearly forty miles to Santa Pueblo. If we make a steady three miles each hour, we shall make it.' He looked doubtfully at the pastor. 'If you are not up to the game, then of course you can ride.'

Faulkner's reaction surprised the captain. He spat in the dust and exclaimed, 'Ride be damned to you! I'll take oath I can keep pace with your troopers.'

'Very well. No offence meant, I'm sure.'

Once they were on their way, the captain fell into step alongside the preacher and said, 'I don't suppose that you would care to favour me with some slight account of your life, sir?'

'Can't be done, my boy,' said Faulkner. 'Just can't be done. I will go so far as to mention that I was not always in the preaching line of business.'

'That I can believe. How did you get those children out of Palo Duro? And how did it come that that Comanchero pursued you alone? Why didn't the whole boiling of them come after you to regain their prisoners?'

'They were most of them dead, Captain. I doubt that you will be troubled by that particular crew again.'

'Dead? Is that a joke?'

'Not in the least. There was a series of what you might describe as unfortunate events. The upshot is that the man your trooper shot was the last of the lot.'

'What happened to them, though? Who killed them?'

'It is a hazardous occupation,' said the preacher, 'buying and selling slaves, gun-running and so on. I would not advise any man to take up such a line of work if he is not able to stand up for himself against all comers. You know

187

what it says in the Good Book: All those that live by the sword shall die by it. Those men must have known when they started trading in innocent young children that they were not likely to die of old age in bed, surrounded by their relatives and friends.'

The young officer looked closely at the man walking beside him. He saw a thin, greying old parson, with maybe only another five or ten years of life left in him. Yet if he was to be believed, this man had single-handedly taken on a group of bandits and killed most of them. 'What will you do when we get to Santa Pueblo?' he asked Faulkner.

'My duty lies in escorting these girls right on to Claremont. Can General Sheridan spare you for such a journey?'

'My instructions are just that, to take those children to Claremont and deliver them to the orphans' asylum.'

'Well then, it looks as though our paths are likely to run side by side for at least the next few days.'

'Tell me, Padre,' said the captain, 'did

you see any signs of activity in the canyon? Did it look to you as though there was trouble brewing?'

'Last night, the Comanche were having a feast. Unless I miss my guess, that means that they will be riding forth this very night. That was always the way of it when I was younger. They would hold a festival and make medicine, then the next evening, that of the full moon, they would go raiding.'

'That is how I read the case, too. The question is, will they head south or north when they leave Palo Duro?'

Pastor Faulkner thought about the matter for a few moments. Then he said, 'I would say south. The Comancheros use Santa Pueblo as a staging post and the Indians are not going to want to queer that pitch. Howsoever, I may be wrong about this.'

'We shall just have to wait and see.'

They marched on at a steady pace for the next few hours without seeing anything untoward. The red sandstone cliffs on their left fell away from the road and they found themselves moving through open country. It was not desert, but nor was it fertile land suitable for farming. It was a dusty, arid plain, with only low, scrubby bushes and a few stunted trees.

There was no chatter now between the soldiers and the children. Everybody in the party appeared to apprehend, without anybody saying it out loud, that it was touch and go whether they would manage to reach Santa Pueblo unmolested. It was now about noon, approaching the hottest time of the day. They could see the rocky crags of Palo Duro away over to their right, perhaps five or ten miles away. Faulkner was looking casually in that direction when he realized that something out on the plain between them and the canyon was also moving along north.

He couldn't be sure what he was seeing, because the ground was shimmery and bright and the heat haze obscured the details, but it looked to him as though it might be a group of riders. They weren't kicking up much dust because, he assumed, the terrain was rockier over that way than it was where they themselves were travelling. The consequence was that while they were probably quite visible to the group moving along on the right, the other riders were only visible if you chanced to be looking in exactly the right direction as he had happened to be doing.

'Captain,' said Faulkner, 'look over yonder, there on the right. I don't know how far off they are, but I can see what looks to be a party of riders moving along with us. It might be a herd of cattle, but my money would be against that.'

'Where do you mean? I can't see anything.'

'See that sharp point in the hills, the little mountain kind of thing? Just to the left of that.'

'You must have better eyes than me. I can't see a thing. Wait, I do see where you mean. How far do you reckon them to be?'

'You are the soldier,' said the preacher

dryly, 'you can hardly call upon a clergy-man to start gauging distances in the field. But I would hazard a guess and say maybe five or six miles. I cannot make out any detail; the heat makes it too hazy.'

'Wait up. I have some field glasses.' The officer raised his voice. 'Halt, now. We might have what you could term uninvited guests. Over on the right, there. Any of you men got sharper eyes than us?' He retrieved his field glasses from the saddle of his horse, which had a perky child of eleven perched atop it. He trained the binoculars on the faint smudge, which was almost out of view.

Meanwhile, one of the troopers was peering through a spyglass. 'It's Indians, Captain,' he announced soberly. 'They're not riding straight at us, but rather moving along in the same direction. They will have seen our dust and I suppose they know of a good place for an ambush.'

'Be quiet, you damned fool,' said the captain in a low, savage tone. 'Do you want to frighten those girls out of their wits? Padre and you, Cartwright, step aside with me over here. We need to decide one or two things.'

The three men walked off from the main group. 'Well,' said Reverend Faulkner, 'what will you do?'

'I do not yet know. Like you, my main concern is to protect those children. The question is, how may we best do so? What are your ideas?'

Trooper Cartwright stared in amazement when he heard his officer asking tactical advice from a preacher. The captain caught the look and said, 'I have not taken leave of my senses, Cartwright. There is more to the reverend gentleman than meets the eye.'

'If you say so, sir,' replied the man dubiously.

'If I were to be asked,' said Faulkner thoughtfully, 'I would say this. Have either of you heard tell of a Prussian soldier called Clausewitz?'

'I seem to recollect the name,' said

the captain, 'when I was at West Point, you know.'

The preacher laughed. 'Forgive me. Well Clausewitz said that the best defence was attack. It is in my mind that we should consider this thought well, when once those riders come close enough for us to see how many there are.'

The sergeant looked again through his spyglass. 'I reckon they're closer than they were. Maybe they are planning to head us off. I can just about see individual horses. I would say that there are perhaps twenty of them, maybe more.'

The cavalry officer looked inquiringly at Pastor Faulkner, who said, 'Kiowa and Comanche are not likely to fight us for the sake of it. They will be determined if we have something worth taking, but otherwise they might not wish to risk their lives just for sport.'

'How does this help us?' asked Sergeant Cartwright. 'They are still sniffing round us and moving in.'

'This is true,' said the preacher patiently. 'If they see those girls, then they will surely fight in order to steal them away and sell them to the Comancheros. At this distance, it is my belief that they will not yet have seen the children, only a line of horses. They probably are not using field glasses. We must get the girls to dismount and get on the far side of the horses, where they cannot be seen. The horses must then close up a bit, to shield them from view.'

The captain clucked in irritation. 'I should have thought of this myself. Cartwright, get the girls off the horses and on the other side from where those Indians are. And then do as the Reverend Faulkner suggests and close ranks a little so that only the horses and troopers can be seen from over there where those Indians are.'

The sergeant saluted and made off to carry out these instructions, but not without first looking a little more closely than he had yet done at the inoffensive-looking minister, whose ideas his commander was apparently so apt to follow.

'Well,' said the captain, ironically, 'have you any other ideas, sir?'

'I think that though this little stratagem might remove from those Indians an urgent motive for setting to with us, I have heard somewhat of your General Sheridan's activities and I do not suppose for a moment that those warriors there are likely to be well disposed in general towards the US cavalry. What do you say to that?'

'You are right, Padre. Even without the attraction of the girls as loot, I would not be surprised if they attack us anyway, just, as you say, for the hell of it.'

'In such a case, we must plan for that eventuality.'

'Well then, what do you recommend?'

'For now? That we keep walking and see how things develop.'

11

Once they were moving again, with the girls now on foot and the troopers back on the horses, Faulkner went to talk to Martha Weiss.

'Well,' said the teacher, 'I suppose you are going to explain to me why those sturdy beggars are now riding and my children are having to trudge along in this heat on foot?'

'Not so loud, ma'am, I don't want to frighten your children. There is a band of Indians, either Kiowa or Comanche, riding alongside us to the right there. We do not want them to see the girls, as it might provide them with a motive to attack us: for plunder, I mean.'

'You think if they do not see the girls, they will leave us alone?'

'It may be so. We must hope for it at least.'

'You don't think so?'

'To speak plainly, Miss Weiss, I do not. They have no reason to love the cavalry at the moment and I believe they outnumber us considerably. In which case, they may just sweep in and try to kill us all for the devilment of it.'

'You are very blunt, Reverend Faulkner. Do you never try to dress up your words a little and set the truth to better advantage?'

'It is not an art I have studied overmuch, ma'am. Perhaps if we get through this little adventure, you might condescend to instruct me in these matters?'

Faulkner could scarcely believe that he was talking in such a way to a woman he had only met a few hours earlier. He was not a man at ease with people usually and that he should be practically flirting with a woman, especially at such a time as this, was very strange and uncommon to him. He felt moved to essay an apology.

'I hope, ma'am, that you do not feel that I am getting above myself with you and being overly familiar? If so, I do apologize. The circumstances are such that normal rules of conduct have, as one might say, flown out of the window. Anyways, I apologize.'

'You've no occasion to. I am well able to handle myself in conversation with a man. You have not upset me or taken liberties. Do not worry; you may be sure that I shall set you straight if you seem to be taking that tack.'

Pastor Faulkner was mulling over her reply when Cartwright came up. 'Begging your pardon, Reverend, ma'am, the captain wonders if you could favour him with your company for a minute?'

'Surely, surely. Miss Weiss, we shall speak again soon, or at least I am sure that I hope so.'

Half the troopers were mounted and the rest were on foot. The five riders and six spare horses gave the impression of a straggling group when viewed from side on. The teacher and her six girls were wholly hidden from view. When he reached the officer, that man handed the preacher his field glasses. Faulkner looked towards the Indians. They were much closer now, so close that he could gain a better idea of their numbers. There were around thirty of them. From the feathers and certain other indications, he took them for Kiowa.

'Well, Captain,' said Pastor Faulkner, 'this is where the knife meets the bone, as we used to say where I was raised. Meaning that the testing time has arrived upon us. If we simply continue as we are, marching on like this, then that party of braves will split up and encircle us. Once they catch sight of those girls, it will be all up with us. They will fight us, we men shall be killed and the girls and their teacher will be taken back to Palo Duro. I do not propose to allow that to happen.'

'Oh you don't, hey?' said the sergeant. 'Perhaps you would tell us how you mean to stop this?'

'I will tell you gladly, my friend,' said the preacher. 'Two of us must stay behind here to guard the children and make sure that the horses are so arranged that they continue to shield them from the view of those marauders over yonder. The rest of us, which will come to seven men, if my figuring is not at fault, will ride out and do battle with the Kiowa. If they do not think that there is any trophy here worth seizing, it may be that they will not be inclined to fight. They may back off from our attack.'

'They may not,' observed the captain. 'They may say, 'We have had enough of those damned bluecoats and seeing as how we outnumber them better than three to one, why don't we massacre every last one of them?' How then?'

'How then?' said Faulkner. 'Why, I don't see that we would be in any worse case than we are currently. I will tell you now, if you men will not accompany me, then I shall ride alone against those Indians. You can wait here for death to overtake you with a certainty or you can join me in a game of bluff.

Are there no poker players here? You are a poor bunch of men if you will not take this hazard.'

It was clear that the soldiers did not take to being chivvied like this by a civilian, and a clergyman at that. Nevertheless, his words had worked something to his purpose on the troopers, because the minister could see that they would not let themselves be outdone in courage by an old preacher. If he rode at the Indians, they would be shamed into taking their places at his side.

'Damn you, Faulkner,' said the officer, with an amused air, 'are you trying to incite mutiny among my men? Have you not heard that this whole area has been declared under martial law? I could put you before a drumhead court martial for this!' He smiled to show that he was only joshing with the preacher. Then he turned to his men. 'Well, how about it, boys? Think it's worth a go?' There were grunts of reluctant assent to a plan which looked likely only to hasten their deaths by a matter of minutes, rather than to save their lives. Still and all, there did not look to be a better scheme on the market and so the captain instructed two men to stay with the horses and children while the other men saddled up.

Pastor Faulkner went back to the teacher. 'Miss Weiss,' he said, 'we are going out to see if we can parlay with those redskins. Here is what I want you to do. If it comes to fighting, and I don't say that this is impossible, then I do not want you and your charges to be at risk of stray bullets. Those two troopers are going to hold the horses in line, so that you will not be seen. All the same, I want you and the children to lie down in the dust, so that you are unlikely to stop some stray bullet that might come this way. The horses will catch most such, but it does no harm to be careful. Will you do this for me?'

The teacher stared intently into Faulkner's face, as though she were reading some difficult and uncertain text which she could barely understand.

Then she nodded and said, 'We will do as you say. I pray God that you might return safely, Reverend Faulkner. I have enjoyed our chats and would not like to think of them being cut short by your untimely death. There, those soldiers are waiting for you. Good luck!' Suddenly, to the preacher's amazement, and also to her own, she darted forward and planted a kiss upon his cheek. Then she blushed and covered her confusion by calling the children to her and getting them to lie down on the ground.

Once he was mounted on Jenny, Faulkner checked the two pistols, which he had had tucked into his belt. Had he but known it, this had given him a very odd character with the soldiers and caused them to wonder if he was really a bandit dressed up as a clergyman or a clergyman tricked out as a bandit. Both weapons had five shots in them. I doubt that I'll get off more than that before this matter resolves itself, he thought to himself.

The Kiowa were now standing off

about a mile and a half away. They had stopped when the cavalry had stopped and did not give the impression that they were in any particular hurry to take action. They were probably wondering what the play was.

'Think they've seen the girls?' the captain said.

'I wouldn't think so for a moment,' replied Faulkner. 'They would be in among us now like foxes in a chicken coop if they thought there was some advantage to be had and something valuable to be stolen. No, it strikes me that these fellows are not sure of the play and cannot decide whether to fight or move on about their business. They are a raiding party; they want booty, not bloodshed.'

'We shall soon see,' said the captain. 'This is sheer madness — six men riding against thirty odd — and I just hope that I have not been buffaloed into it by you, Reverend Faulkner.'

'At least this way, we have a chance of saving those children. Otherwise, once they circled round and caught a sight of them, we would all be dead in any case. This gives us a chance, even if it is as slender as a hair. Men were more apt to hazard their lives when I was young and that's a fact. Odds of five to one is nothing; I do not know what is wrong with you youngsters. Captain,' said Faulkner jovially, 'I think it would be more fitting if you were to give the order to ride off.'

'Thank you, Reverend Faulkner. I am obliged to you for acknowledging my authority. Come on, boys, let's be going.'

The six troopers and the clergyman rode off at a trot, not in a column, but side by side. The Indians still made no move, which raised Pastor Faulkner's spirits and confirmed him in his suspicions — that these men had been heading elsewhere and had only stopped out of curiosity to see what the army were up to so near to the canyons. The question was, would they fight if attacked?

There was no more than half a mile

to go when Faulkner said to the officer, 'Well, are you going to give the order to gallop? At this rate we shall be trotting around them like a display of dressage riders. We want them to know that we mean business and are after their blood. They have seen nothing yet to scare them.'

'They might yet break and run,' said the captain. 'I do not like to be crowded into taking decisions. You are not in the army, you know. You are only a civilian.'

'I have got you this far. Let's see if I can get you to show some gumption now.'

With that and without saying another word, Faulkner spurred on the mare into a canter and then a gallop. He heard from behind, the captain's voice crying faintly, 'Faulkner, you bastard! Come back here now, you mad fool!' By this time, he was only a hundred yards from the braves, who were still watching him impassively, not looking as if they cared a damn for this crazed white man. This wouldn't do at all; they did not look like men who even knew that they were under attack. The preacher drew the Navy Colt from his belt and fired twice into the mass of men. He had the satisfaction of seeing one man cry out and fall from his horse.

As he began shooting, Pastor Faulkner became aware that he was no longer alone and that either side of him were two cavalrymen. They, too, began firing their pistols. There were shots from behind as well, as the other four soldiers joined the melee. What puzzled the minister was that the Indians were not firing back and it was only as he was within ten or twenty yards and started to veer off to one side, that he saw the reason for this. With all the gun-running taking place in and around Palo Duro, he and the soldiers had taken it as a matter of course that any tribesmen they encountered would be bearing firearms. These men, though, had only lances, knives and bows.

What had looked at the beginning to be liable to end in a massacre of the white men was turning now into a massacre of quite another sort. The seven men were pouring shot after shot into the Indians, who retaliated with a few arrows and lances. Then they fled, leaving behind seven of their number, who had been killed. Four horses also lay dying before the shooting subsided. It had been a one-sided affair indeed, but not in the way that they had expected when they set off on the charge.

The officer looked a little annoyed, which Faulkner could well understand. It is not many commanders of a troop of cavalry who delight in seeing their authority usurped by an aging clergyman. Still, his actions had achieved the end upon which he had set out. They trotted back to where the two troopers were guarding the girls.

The girls were placed back on the horses and the group was about to set off again to Santa Pueblo, when the captain called Pastor Faulkner aside for a little private consultation, out of earshot of the others.

'Reverend, I will need to make out a report on the skirmish which we just undertook. I am not about to explain at length how you took over what should have been a scouting party and helped start a massacre of Indians who, as far as I can see, would not have been any threat to us.'

'Well, son,' said Faulkner, 'you did not appear to think that riding out to them was a bad idea.'

The officer gave him an angry look. 'As I say, I will not include your name in those who took part in that sortie. Apart from all else, I am not sure that General Sheridan would wish me to allow a clergyman to fight alongside the US cavalry in this way. But I blame you, sir, for those deaths. You are very much to blame for what occurred. Had it not been for your galloping on ahead like that and opening fire, it is my belief that those Kiowa might have broken and fled. Their deaths are on your conscience, Faulkner, not mine.'

'Truth is, we were both to blame. You had no business letting me railroad you into an attack in the first place. But if you want to salve your conscience in this way, that is fine by me. Rescuing these children has turned into a bloody affair, I will not deny it. However, those who first snatched them must bear the responsibility for the bulk of what has followed. If those girls had arrived at the Claremont Orphans' Asylum as planned, there would have been no need for me to go on the scout like this.'

'I have remarked before, Reverend Faulkner, that you are a damned odd sort of preacher. Tell me, how long have you been in the religious line of work?'

'That does not signify. I will not lay out my life's history for your edification. I am a man of God and will do what is needful to protect the widow and orphan. Those that set out to harm a bunch of orphans had best take care that the lightning does not descend upon them. I will not stand by and see

211

such goings on.'

'I will say, sir, that it has been interesting knowing you, but that I would not like to spend too much time in your company. I find service in the army quite lively enough without men like you to complicate matters.'

Faulkner gave a sudden laugh. 'I am sorry for starting that fight. I can say no more than that. Mind, you being a soldier and all, I should not have thought that a little shooting would have upset you so much. You are too squeamish, perhaps. We have not fallen out, I hope?' He reached out his hand and the young captain took it, shaking his head ruefully as he did so.

'I hope, Reverend Faulkner, that I do not have the misfortune to find myself riding alongside another Presbyterian minister in a hurry. The breed is a mite too troublesome for me.'

As they moved off, Faulkner fell into step beside Martha Weiss. She addressed him, saying, 'Well, sir, I suppose that you are feeling pretty satisfied with the way that things have turned out so far?'

'I would not say that I am satisfied, no. There have been a few too many deaths for me to feel anything much but regret about the turn things have taken since I left Claremont. It was all done for the sake of those girls, but I will confess to you, Miss Weiss, that when I am out and about with a gun at hand, things often take a course of this nature. It would be a better thing for the world if the swords were to be beaten into ploughshares, as it says in scripture.'

'Don't take on so. You did what you had to. Those six girls will bless your name all their lives for what you have done for them. I do not approve of killing and such, but all the same, I don't think you need to lose too much sleep. All the men you have killed were armed, were they not?'

'You are a great comfort to me, ma'am, a great comfort. Yes, it is the fact that I have only killed men who were looking for trouble and had weapons in their hands. I have not gone out to look for violence, except for that little affair with those Indians just now. Even they were armed, though, and I have an idea that they meant mischief and were simply surprised to be met with such a vigorous response.'

'What did that officer make of the business? I had an impression that he would not be engaging to write you any glowing testimonial?'

'He thinks I buffaloed him into attacking the Kiowa.'

'And did you?'

'Why, ma'am, you are a regular cross-examiner! I was in court once and the attorney questioned me in this wise.'

'What's the answer?'

'I think he lacked the resolve to mount a spirited attack. I kind of helped matters along and got his men worked up, I suppose. He was annoyed about it.'

The children were beginning to get a little fretful, with the sun beating down upon them and the unfamiliar experience of riding horseback. A five-minute walk around a paddock is one thing for a child who is not used to horses, but a long journey in the boiling hot sun with no food and little water is quite a different matter. The preacher eyed the girls closely and then said to their teacher, 'Are any of those children the sort to become hysterical or have fainting fits or anything of that nature? If so, we need to attend to her and head off anything of the sort. In my experience, once one of a group of girls starts off down that road, her companions are apt to follow.'

Martha Weiss eyed her girls grimly. 'Don't worry about that, Pastor Faulkner. No girl that I have had the care of has ever yet succumbed to anything of the sort. I shall keep an eye out.'

They reached Santa Pueblo at about eleven that night and soldiers, girls, woman and preacher were altogether beat. There were few lights on, except at the cantina, and so the cavalry commandeered a barn whose owner was still up and about. On seeing the tired girls, he offered freely that they could all sleep in the hay if they wanted. It was a tight squeeze with eight soldiers, one teacher, six girls and a clergyman, but they made themselves as comfortable as possible. The girls and their teacher took the hayloft and the men arranged themselves as best they could on the ground, strewing hay around to make their sleep a little more comfortable. Faulkner drifted off almost at once and slept deeply until first light, when he was awakened by a sharp, metallic click a few inches from his ear. He opened his eyes to find himself staring down the barrel of a cocked revolver.

12

The pistol was being held by a grimy-looking, unshaven man of about thirty, who indicated by placing a finger to his lips that Faulkner should make no noise but get up and accompany him. The soldiers were all sound asleep and the preacher did not feel inclined to put the man to the test by raising the alarm. His own two pistols lay nearby, but he would be unlikely to be able to snatch one up before he was shot.

The two of them walked out of the barn and into the area behind Santa Pueblo's main street. The man marched Faulkner to the livery stable. Inside, there was a small storeroom, which the man with the pistol ordered him to enter. He then said, 'Thought you could just come to our town and shoot a man down, did you? I didn't think you would be foolish enough to return here, but then doesn't it say in the Bible that the criminal always returns to the scene of his crime?'

Pastor Faulkner shook his head. 'The closest I can recollect tending towards such a notion is the second book of Peter, chapter two, verse twenty-two, 'as a dog returneth to his own vomit'. If you wished to discuss scripture, you hardly needed to abduct me at gunpoint, though. It is my job to do so.'

'You like a joke. Perhaps I should tell you that I am what passes for law in this town. I am a deputy and it is my business to look into shooting and suchlike. Couple of nights ago, there was a man shot. You left the next day and I have cause to think you were concerned in the shooting.'

'Where is your warrant or at least your badge?'

'I do not have to answer to you. The boot is all on the other foot. Some friends of mine have been deputed to take you to Oneida for an official investigation. Till then, I shall keep you locked here.' With that, the man closed the door and secured it with a padlock.

It did not sound to the preacher that this was a true bill. Even if the man was a deputy sheriff, it was likely that he was being paid to surrender him up to a group of the dead man's friends, who would then escort him peacefully out of town and then, when they were alone, hang him from the nearest tree. Evidently, the man he had killed here had friends who were desirous of avenging themselves for their comrade's death.

Some little time later, Pastor Faulkner heard footsteps and the sound of angry voices. He supposed that the time had arrived when the friends of the man he had shot in this town were coming to take him away and execute judgment upon him. The door of the storeroom opened and he was astonished to see Sergeant Cartwright standing there with his pistol drawn. He winked at Faulkner and said, 'Come on out now, you old villain.'

The captain and three of his men stood there, disputing with the man who claimed to be a deputy. The captain said, 'This is a military matter. This man is my prisoner and I aim to take him north for a court martial.'

The deputy said angrily, 'What am I to do? I have promised to send him south. I will look a fool.'

'I do not know what game you are playing,' said the officer softly, 'but it is a very dangerous one. This whole area, including this town, has been declared under martial law by the federal army. If you impede me in any way, I can have you up before a court martial as well. You do know that? We are taking this man and that is an end to the matter.'

'I shall send word to Oneida. I will make trouble for you with your superiors.'

The captain took a couple of paces closer to the man and said, almost in a whisper, 'If you do that, I promise you that the army will move into this town and use it as their base. We will quarter here for the winter and commandeer whatever we take a fancy to. None of those Comancheros will be able to fart without the cavalry hearing of it. I don't think your friends will thank you for bringing about that state of affairs. What do you think?'

'I do not believe you have the authority.'

'Just try me and I tell you now that the cavalry will be down on this place like a duck on a June bug.'

'What has the man done that the army want him?'

'That's no affair of yours. Just keep your mouth shut, don't cause ructions and if you are lucky, this pesthole will continue to be overlooked.'

The man who had detained Faulkner shrugged and ambled out of the barn. The captain turned to Faulkner and said, 'You surely are a whole lot of trouble, Padre. I have never known a man slip so easily in and out of danger. It will be a great relief to me to unload you and those children in Claremont. I have never had a mission that caused me so many problems. I would sooner face a dozen Comanche braves than deal with a man like you again. Come on. I don't want to hang round here longer than can be helped.'

The final stage of the journey to Claremont promised to be a good deal more pleasant than that from Palo Duro. Provisions were acquired along with a cart for carrying the girls and their teacher. Although the army had little enough cash money with them, they had authority to requisition what they needed and then leave the owners a chit, which could later be redeemed with the army commissariat. The civilians would not lose by the arrangement. They left Santa Pueblo that morning, with the preacher nominally a prisoner of the army. He was riding Jenny and did his best to look dejected as they passed through the town.

A short while after they had left the town behind them, the officer rode up and returned Faulkner's guns to him. He was disposed to be talkative and the pastor felt that he owed it to the man to be civil and sociable, notwithstanding the fact that he was feeling quiet and thoughtful and not in the mood for casual conversation.

'Do you think that fellow really was a deputy?' asked the captain.

'It's possible. Even so, I think he was in the pay of friends of a man who fell foul of me a couple of nights ago. I think the aim was to get me out of sight of the town and hang me.'

'What do you mean, the man 'fell foul' of you? What befell him?'

'He was killed,' said Faulkner shortly.

'Well, you have at least ensured the safety of those girls. I was hoping to be able to stage a daring rescue mission on my own account, but you rather spiked my guns there. I never was so surprised in the whole course of my life when we came to the top of those cliffs and found you leading those children along the road.'

'I dare say that you will be able to draft your report to the general so that your role in the affair looks bigger than was the case. I would rather have my name left out of things, anyway. It would not do for a respectable clergyman to be getting a reputation for such goings on.'

They didn't reach Claremont that day. The cart made for slow travelling and they needed to stop from time to time while various girls were sick from the motion of the thing. There was not a member of that whole entire party who was not longing to sleep in a soft bed as soon as it might prove possible to do so.

They camped out and started a fire to cook food and boil up coffee. When the government was picking up the bill, the soldiers tended to be free with their promissory notes and they had not stinted themselves in their requisitions. Despite their weariness, there was a good deal of jollity, with the cavalrymen teasing the girls and the girls enjoying the attention of the men.

The girls were none too keen to

spend yet another night sleeping rough, but there was little that could be done about it. The troopers offered various things like blankets and so on to make them more comfortable, but everybody was a little scratchy and out of spirits at having to camp out again.

When they moved off the next morning, the preacher rode alongside the cart and spoke to Martha Weiss. 'We should arrive in Claremont by midday and I will direct you to the orphanage. Your girls are still expected and provision has been made for them. I hope that they may not have to stay there long, because there are plenty of farmers who are willing to take children of this age into their homes in return for help around the place.'

'You would not let anybody mistreat them or overwork them?' asked the teacher.

Faulkner looked at her indignantly. 'I would not, ma'am. There is not one child gone out of that orphanage whose welfare I do not visit and check up on. I am up to all the games of using orphans as slave labour, as happens in some places. Not round here, ma'am, not while I have breath in my body.'

'I'm sorry,' she said quietly. 'I feel protective of those girls. I did not mean to cause any offence.'

'None taken, none at all.'

'Will there be a room for me to stay at the orphans' asylum, just for a night or two? I have not made any particular arrangements yet for where I am to go after I have seen those girls settled.'

The preacher cleared his throat and then said in a low voice, 'I have a large house and there is a spare room. It is for visitors, but I have never had one since I have lived there.'

Martha Weiss cut in quickly. 'You have never had a visitor to stay? How long have you lived there?'

'I couldn't rightly say. Eleven years, perhaps.'

'Eleven years and never a soul to come and stay with you? That must have made for a lonely life.'

'That's neither here nor there,' he said stiffly. 'What I was about to say was that if you wished to favour me with your company, then you are more than welcome to have that spare room for just as long as you might wish to stay.' He was suddenly horrified in case she thought that he was suggesting something improper. 'My housekeeper, Mrs O'Hara, lives with me, so it is not as though I would be asking you to share a house with me, with just the two of us in it, if you see what I mean . . . There will be a chaperone, so to speak.'

To Pastor Faulkner's great confusion, the young woman threw back her head and laughed long and loud. 'You will be the death of me, Reverend Faulkner. Here we are, having been travelling rough, sleeping in barns together and under carts, witnessing murder and I don't know what all else together and you are worried that our reputations will be damaged because I stay in your guest room? Lord, but you are a strange one.'

'There is one more thing, ma'am. I am not asking you to tell a lie for me. For my own part, I shall simply intimate that while on my short vacation, I chanced across you and the girls, you having been rescued by the cavalry. I am happy for them to have any honour and glory which might attach to the business. I would be obliged if you could leave my name out of anything you yourself have to say on the subject. It is up to you, though, I would scruple to urge you to tell a direct falsehood.'

'You need not be uneasy about that. I doubt anybody would believe my own account in any case. You are right, far better to leave the plaudits to those brave boys in blue. I cannot answer for the girls, though.'

'They will chatter, but I doubt anybody will pay heed to them if they say that one of the trustees at the orphanage was conducting himself like a bandit chief. Do not worry about that.'

The teacher looked at Faulkner and

paused for moment, before saying, 'I should be pleased and delighted to stay at your house, Pastor Faulkner. Thank you.'

Their arrival at Claremont — the girls from Oneida, accompanied by a troop of cavalry and their own minister from the Presbyterian Church — created a minor sensation. The sudden disappearance of the pastor from the church had been remarked upon in the little town and there had been those who hinted darkly that there was more to the case than met the eye. Their suspicions were not of wholesale murder, though; more that that upright and puritanical man might have been caught with his accounts not in order or perhaps detected in an affair with one of his parishioners. He had been a permanent fixture on the streets of the town for so long that suddenly vanishing in that way had been bound to cause gossip.

After installing the six girls at the orphanage, it took Pastor Faulkner that the correct thing would be to let the elders know that he was back in town and would be resuming his duties with immediate effect. He had been gone less than a week, but could already sense that the community was beginning to slip. There was nothing like a sober minister patrolling the streets to remind folk of their duties and obligations both to the Deity and also to the weaker members of their community.

Mrs O'Hara was pleased to see him, but also surprised. Her surprise at seeing him back so soon was as nothing, though, compared with the shock of hearing that for the first time ever, he was having a guest to stay. And a lady, too! Faulkner left the house hastily to avoid the flurry of activity by which his housekeeper signalled her readiness to entertain a visitor for a few nights.

He found Martha Weiss at the orphans' asylum, making the girls comfortable and introducing them to the other children there. She came up to him when he entered the ward, saying, 'Pastor Faulkner, have you yet repented of your rash invitation for me to spend a night or two as your guest?'

He smiled, in a more natural way than he was wont to do before his little excursion. 'Not a bit of it, Miss Weiss. Everything is in hand and if you will just be a little more patient, I shall call back in an hour, after I have taken care of a small matter of business.'

She leaned forward and said, almost in a whisper, 'I am glad to observe that you have shed those pistols. Does this mean that your business on this occasion will not entail shooting or blowing anybody up?'

'Do not joke about death,' he said reprovingly. 'This is by way of being a pastoral visit.'

'Hurry back. I am eager to see you in your own home. I cannot really get used to you in your capacity as a respectable clergyman, but I dare say I will get used to it by and by.'

The ride out to the Carson place

took only twenty minutes. Billy Wilson was working in the vegetable garden but ran up to the preacher as soon as he caught sight of him. 'Have you come to talk to my step-pa about Sunday School, Pastor Faulkner? They said that you had gone away and I was afeared that you would not be coming back again.'

Faulkner smiled down at the boy and said, 'When I say I'll do a thing, Billy, you may rest assured that I shall do it. Remember that principle as you grow up and you will not go far wrong. Let your word be your bond. Where's your step-pa, over yonder in the fields?'

'Yes, sir. Do you want me to lead you there?'

'No, I can find my own way. You just carry on and I will see you at church on Sunday.'

Pastor Faulkner found Joe Carson, a hard-faced and ill-favoured man in his late thirties, hoeing a field. He looked up when Faulkner approached and stopped working. 'I hope you ain't looking for any contributions towards the church steeple fund or whatever else you are begging after at this moment? I have not a cent to spare for such foolishness.'

'This has no reference to money, Mr Carson. I am calling to remind you that your stepson has been a faithful member of the church for some time and I am hoping that he will continue on that road. By which I mean, be sure to give him the Sabbath off and allow him to come to Sunday School and meet his friends.'

Carson dropped the hoe and walked right up close to the preacher, perhaps meaning to crowd him. 'What the hell's it got to do with you?'

''A soft answer turneth away wrath, but harsh words provoketh a rebuke.' Proverbs, fifteen, verse one.'

'Don't come on my farm, preaching to me. The boy needs to work. His ma was too soft on him until we married. He must toughen up.'

The sight of this swaggering bully,

who thought that he could lord it over a 10-year-old boy, was too much for the minister. He grabbed hold of Carson's shirt-front and walked forward, causing the man to scrabble with his feet to avoid falling over backwards. 'Listen, Carson,' he said in a quiet and reasonable way, 'I have had what you might term a trying few days and my patience is all wore away. This would not be a good day to get crosswise to me. Do you apprehend my meaning?'

Joe Carson stood stock-still, suddenly in fear of the old man about whom he had made so many contemptuous jokes in the past. 'All right, Parson, there's no need to get agitated. I did not realize that this was such an important matter to you.'

'Just let that boy have a break on Sundays, you son of a bitch, or you and me are going be falling out with each other. I do not think that either of us want that.'

The preacher released the front of Carson's shirt and stepped back a pace or two to ease up the tension. It was clear that Joe Carson was taken aback by the entire episode and he stood there looking uncertainly at Faulkner. After a pause, he said, 'Ah, what the hell. Let the boy come to your damned church if he's that keen. Tell you the truth, he ain't much use in the fields, anyways.'

Pastor Faulkner said courteously, 'That is right good of you, Mr Carson. I am obliged to you and I know that Billy will thank you for your change of heart. You have a good day, now.' He turned and walked back to the house, where Billy was waiting with his horse.

'Well, Pastor?'

'I reasoned with your step-pa, Billy and he saw things in my light. You will be coming to Sunday School. Mind you thank him properly, now, you hear me?'

'Thanks, Pastor Faulkner.'

13

That night, Pastor Faulkner dined with Martha Weiss in his own home. Mrs O'Hara was at her most agreeable and provided a perfectly good meal for them. The preacher had freshened up and changed into another suit of clothes. The same could not be said for the teacher, though, who had lost her bag when she was taken by the Kiowa.

'Will you let me provide you with a little money to buy some new clothes, Miss Weiss?' Faulkner asked tentatively, hoping that he was not overstepping the bounds of decency. He had a vague notion that no respectable woman accepted gifts of clothing from a man. 'There would be no hurry to repay me.'

'I cannot trespass too much upon your good nature, Pastor Faulkner. Folk will say that I am taking advantage of you.'

'I don't care much what folk say. Will you let me buy some clothes?'

'Thank you, you are very kind. You know, seeing you like this on your home ground, you are a very different man from the one I saw at Palo Duro. I cannot think that you would behave in an aggressive manner here.'

'You would think not. I must get back more into this quieter way of comporting myself. I nearly slipped into bad ways soon after we returned.'

'How's that?' asked the teacher. 'What happened?'

He told her about the run-in with Joe Carson and she listened with amusement. At the end, she said, 'You need somebody to take care of you. You will grow old and crabby if you live alone for too much longer.'

When they had parted after dinner, Pastor Faulkner fell to his knees in his room and said, 'Lord, I have not felt this way for many years. I cannot hope that a woman like that might feel anything at all for a wretch like me. All the same, I must say something to her. You must advise me on this matter and give me a sign of what you think. I cannot stop thinking of that teacher and if she stays here any longer, I am sure to let my feelings be known. Help me, Lord, and guide me in this matter. Amen.'

The end of our story is almost in sight. To finish matters up, Martha Weiss spent a week in the minister's house before he plucked up the courage to speak his mind. The teacher herself also suffered agonies during this time, unable to decide whether Jonas Faulkner cared for her as a woman, or if she was just another charity case to him, like Billy Wilson or the girls from the Oneida orphanage. When he finally opened his mind to her, she was dumbstruck with the force of his affection.

The minister from the Presbyterian Church and the teacher from Oneida were married in late August. They had both felt it fitting that once they had declared their love for one another, she should move out of his house until the wedding. There would be tongues enough wagging when it became known that the pastor was going to marry a woman who had just lately been staying in his house. The circumstances of his vacation had also raised questions in the minds of some, with the way that he suddenly arrived back with a young woman in tow, who he at once installed in his home. There was, some people said, more to the case than met the eye.

The wedding at the First Claremont Presbyterian Church was well attended, not only by the regular congregation, but also by many who were just curious to see old sober-sides the preacher getting hitched up to a pretty young woman. How their life developed and what chanced in the years to come, there is no room to tell, and so we must end with the happy couple leaving the church and heading off for their honeymoon on a sunny August day in 1868.

We do hope that you have enjoyed reading this large print book.

Did you know that all of our titles are available for purchase?

We publish a wide range of high quality large print books including:
Romances, Mysteries, Classics
General Fiction
Non Fiction and Westerns

Special interest titles available in large print are:
The Little Oxford Dictionary
Music Book, Song Book
Hymn Book, Service Book

Also available from us courtesy of Oxford University Press:
Young Readers' Dictionary
(large print edition)
Young Readers' Thesaurus
(large print edition)

For further information or a free brochure, please contact us at:
Ulverscroft Large Print Books Ltd.,
The Green, Bradgate Road, Anstey,
Leicester, LE7 7FU, England.
Tel: (00 44) 0116 236 4325
Fax: (00 44) 0116 234 0205

GUN STORM

Corba Sunman

Death comes calling on the small mining town of Lodestone when the storekeeper's wife Martha is murdered by a thief. Deputy Jim Donovan pursues and guns down a man witnessed fleeing the scene, but testimony from his brother Joey indicates that the killer is still at large. Elroy Johnson, the stagecoach robber Donovan arrested three years ago, is back in town — could he be involved? Meanwhile, the outlaw Stomp Cullen and his gang have been spotted lurking around Lodestone. All signs point to an upcoming gun storm . . .

SKYHORSE

John Ladd

Judge Nathan Berkley requests a seemingly simple task of his adopted son, Appaloosa King: ride to the remote town of Deadlock to pick up Catherine, the judge's newly-discovered daughter. Trouble starts when, on the way, King leads his two cowboys off on a diversion, aiming to meet up with a mysterious messenger — who, unbeknownst to the trio, has a deadly reason for the rendezvous. All looks lost until a stranger arrives on the scene — the man known as Skyhorse . . .